Death of a Nurse

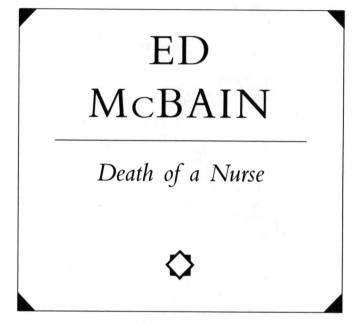

ED McBAIN

Death of a Nurse

THE ARMCHAIR DETECTIVE LIBRARY

A DIVISION OF
OTTO PENZLER BOOKS
NEW YORK

This work was originally published as *Murder in the Navy* under the pseudonym Richard Marsten.

Introduction copyright © 1994 by HUI Corporation
Copyright © 1955 by Fawcett Publications, Inc.
Copyright renewed by Evan Hunter, 1983

This edition is reprinted by arrangement with the author.

Otto Penzler Books
129 W. 56th Street
New York, NY 10019
(Editorial Offices only)

Macmillan Publishing Company   Maxwell Macmillan Canada, Inc.
866 Third Avenue   1200 Eglinton Avenue East, Suite 200
New York, NY 10022   Don Mills, Ontario M3C 3N1

Macmillan Publishing Company is part of the Maxwell Communication Group of Companies.

Library of Congress Cataloging-in-Publication Data
McBain, Ed, 1926–
    Death of a nurse / by Ed McBain.
        p.   cm.
    "Originally published as *Murder in the navy* under the pseudonym
Richard Marsten"—T.p. verso.
    ISBN 1-56287-061-0 (trade ed.). — ISBN 1-56287-062-9 (limited ed.)
    I. Title.
PS3515.U585D43   1994   93-49477   CIP
813'.54—dc20

Otto Penzler Books are available at special discounts for bulk purchases for sales promotions, premiums, fund-raising, or educational use. For details, contact:

Special Sales Director
Macmillan Publishing Company
866 Third Avenue
New York, NY 10022

10 9 8 7 6 5 4 3 2 1

Printed in the United States of America

This one is for Harry—
my father-in-law

NOTE

There is no ship in the United States fleet named the U.S.S. *Sykes,* nor does any destroyer carry the designating numbers 012. The ship in these pages, therefore, is not intended as a representation of any actual United States Naval vessel, since, to the best of the author's knowledge, there has never been a homicide committed aboard a ship of the United States Navy. In like manner, no attempt has been made to reconstruct the actual physical characteristics of either the nurses' quarters or the base hospital at Norfolk, Virginia. The characters, too, are all fictional and the opinions they express are not necessarily those of the author.

INTRODUCTION

Actually, this isn't such a bad book.

I say this objectively because I've just finished reading it for the first time since I wrote it, and that was a good many moons ago. The way I figure the chronology:

The contract with Fawcett Publications for a book then titled *The Dead Nurse* (my original title) is dated January 7, 1955, when you and I were young, Maggie. It is between the publisher and "Evan Hunter writing under the pseudonym of Richard Marsten." The book was published for the first time by Fawcett's Gold Medal Books in August of 1955. This was ten months after publication of *The Blackboard Jungle*, the novel that marked the big leap forward in Evan Hunter's writing career, a mere *six* months after the release of the blockbuster MGM movie based on that novel. In other words, *The Dead Nurse* (or *Murder in the Navy*, as Fawcett retitled it without a by-your-leave) was actually written *before* I wrote *The Blackboard Jungle*, but it did not find a publisher until *after* that book was published. It should therefore come as no surprise that when *this* book was first published, the cover looked like this:

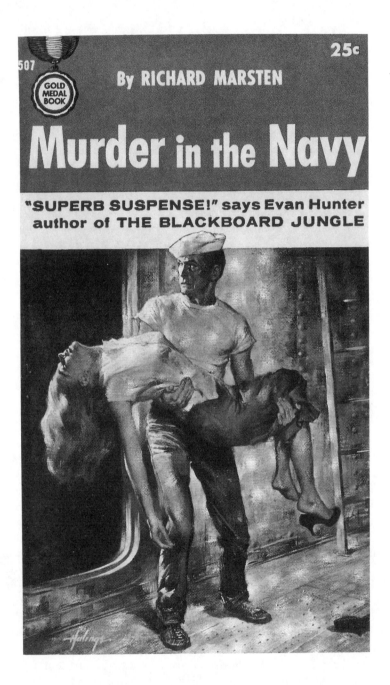

507

25c

GOLD MEDAL BOOK

By RICHARD MARSTEN

Murder in the Navy

"SUPERB SUSPENSE!" says Evan Hunter author of THE BLACKBOARD JUNGLE

To its eternal embarrassment, Fawcett exhibited not the slightest scintilla of shame when it asked Evan Hunter to provide a quote for the poor struggling novelist named Richard Marsten, which pseudonym, by the way, had been coined from the given names of Hunter's three sons, Richard, Mark, and Ted. It is further interesting to note that Hunter himself did not even have the good grace to blush when, in fact, he *did* provide the quote. He did not feel he was revealing the more venal side of his nature, you see. Instead, he thought he recognized a good inside joke when he saw one. It would be nice to report that Hunter's covert recommendation resulted in astounding sales for *Murder in the Navy*. It did not.

However, the saga continues.

In December of 1970, to prove that publishers are forever and always grasping, Fawcett offered Hunter a "formal and binding amendment to the contract entered into on January 7, 1955," providing that "in place of the pseudonym of Richard Marsten, your pseudonym in the revived edition of *Murder in the Navy* will be Ed McBain."

Presumably Fawcett meant to say "*on* the revived edition," but the publisher's intentions were nonetheless clear for any perceptive reader to grasp. Hunter had become a so-called "serious" novelist by then, and could not possibly allow his august name to appear as author of a mere "mystery." McBain, on the other hand, had been building a shoddy reputation as a mystery writer, so why not take advantage of his notoriety and stick *his* name on a new edition of the book? Before anyone could say, "if the foregoing is in concert with your understanding of the chain of arrangements that have been exercised with regard to this property," the deed was done. It would be further nice to report that McBain's name on the cover resulted in skyrocketing sales. It did not.

Nonetheless, the book, as heretofore noted, is a pretty good one. Considering the fact that I hadn't written too many mysteries *before* this one . . .

My memory is that there were two Evan Hunter mysteries respectively titled *The Evil Sleep* and *Don't Crowd Me,* and a Richard Marsten mystery titled *Runaway Black,* all written before *The Dead Nurse* or *Murder in the Navy* or *Death of a Nurse,* as it was finally retitled a few years ago. The reason I wanted the word *nurse* in the title from the very beginning, by the way, was that I was told by a man named Herb Alexander, a good friend and the then-editor-in-chief at Pocket Books, Inc., that any title with the word *nurse* in it automatically sold 50 percent more copies. Fawcett, grasping but essentially unaware, did not recognize the pulling power of this single word. Neither did the reading public; like Hunter and McBain before it, *nurse* did not appreciably boost sales. I pass the word on now, willingly and free of charge, to any other mercenary publisher who may wish to take advantage of its potency.

Both of the Evan Hunter mysteries were simply awful.

The Evil Sleep was about a drug addict who wakes up with a dead blonde (or brunette or redhead, I forget which, Harold, this was forty *years* ago) in bed with him. Essentially a Man-on-the-Run novel, it dealt with the hero's desperate attempts to get his next fix while the police are looking for him. *Don't Crowd Me* was an Innocent-Bystander-cum-Man-on-the-Run novel. Advertising man goes up to Lake George for the week (or the weekend, I forget which) and finds Guess What in his cabin? Yep, another dead blonde. Or brunette or redhead. He has to find the true killer in order to prove his innocence before all those hick cops up there throw him in jail for the rest of his natural life.

Runaway Black was a straightforward Man-on-the-Run novel (what *else* could it be with that title?), frankly influenced by the movie *Odd Man Out,* which I'd probably seen just before I began writing it. An interesting sidelight on this title is that the most recent publisher to contract for the book flatly refused to call it *Runaway Black* on the ground that the word *Black* might offend people. I reminded them that when I wrote the book, the term *Negro* was then in vogue, and that until recently the designation *Black* was entirely acceptable. I asked if perhaps they wished to retitle the book *Runaway African-American,* in keeping with today's fashion.

What they'd entirely forgotten, of course, was the fact that I'd written the book in a black man's voice, and was enormously pleased when most reviewers felt a black man had actually written it. I told the publishers that to my knowledge my credentials were impeccable, but if they were terrified of using the word *Black* in a title, then perhaps they should look deeper into their *own* hearts. They cancelled the contract. I did not have to return the advance. The book will be published soon by another house not as concerned by whatever may be considered chic for the moment. I am still very proud of *Runaway Black.* Coincidentally, it is the book that immediately preceded *Death of a Nurse.* The book after that was *The Blackboard Jungle,* in which a black student is the co-hero, a character memorialized by Sidney Poitier in the film.

The astute reader will have noticed *many* "politically incorrect" expressions or actions in *Death of a Nurse.* Today, I would not have written a scene in which anyone finds a drunk cute or attractive. I would not have written about people forever lighting up cigarettes. I would not have included all those macho sailors whistling or leering at poor Jean Dvorak. Today, I certainly would not write the words "the taut ribbing of her stockings, the garters biting into her flesh," a holdover from my apprentice days in the pulp magazines. Nor would I silhouette a woman against sunlight with such alarming frequency, the better to see her outlined legs, m'dear. Nor—*perish* the thought—would I ever call a woman a "girl."

I never discussed any of these ancient attitudes or fashions with my present publisher, the equally venal but enormously astute Mr. Otto Penzler. I'm assuming he feels the way I do, that the record should stand. This was the way I was writing back then, for better or worse. Regarding Jean Dvorak, however, I don't think I felt completely comfortable writing about women until I wrote *Mothers and Daughters* in 1960, when I deliberately set myself the task of writing almost entirely from the viewpoints of three generations of women. *Death of a Nurse* preceded that one by six years. I was still learning. Forgive me.

When Otto asked me if there was a non–87th Precinct novel I would like to see reprinted in hardcover, I immediately suggested this book. I believe this is the first time it's appeared in hardcover in the United States, although there was a British hardcover edition published in 1972, wherein the word *bloody* was magically repeated with some regularity. On the jacket flap of that edition, the following invitation appeared:

"If you have enjoyed this book, please write and tell us. There are probably many others which will afford you equal pleasure, and we will be most happy to send you our latest list."

So what are you waiting for?

Ed McBain
Norwalk, Connecticut
June 1994

Death of a Nurse

1

HE SAT ON THE PORT SIDE OF THE SHIP, JUST OUTSIDE THE
radar shack and the ladder leading up to the bridge. He sat
on an ammunition box, and he rested one hand on the
20-millimeter antiaircraft gun, which was uncovered now
because the ship had visitors.

He was wearing undress blues, as the Old Man had
ordered. He didn't like undress blues, because the sleeves
were short and had no cuffs, and he really felt that dress
blues would have been more fitting for Navy Day. He kept
an eye peeled for officers because he knew he'd be chewed
out if anyone saw him just sitting here when the ship was
swarming with visitors. But he didn't want to miss her
when she came aboard, and his perch just below the bridge
gave him a full view of the approach to the dock.

There were two other ships tied up at the dock, and he
looked over at them now. One was a battleship, and it
squatted on the waterline like a big gray hotel. The other
was a submarine, and it seemed to attract most of the
visitors, but he supposed that was natural. He had to admit
his own ship, a destroyer, looked smart enough. There
was a man on either side of the gangway, each wearing a
guard belt, each holding a rifle at Parade Rest. An Army
major walked up the dock, heading for the two men with
their hats neatly squared, the dull blue barrels of the rifles
angled forward. When the major reached the gangway,
both men sprang to attention, the rifles snapping back
against their thighs, their left hands with palms flat cross-
ing to touch the muzzles of the guns in salute.

The major returned the salute and started up the gangway.

Maybe she won't come, he thought.

The thought made him uncomfortable, and he slid off the ammo box and began pacing the deck. The ship bobbed gently with the motion of the water. He saw Mr. Haverford starting down the port side of the ship, resplendent in his carefully tailored blues, wearing a new hat with the braid glistening at its peak. He ducked quickly into the passageway, stayed there for several moments, and then went out to stand near the gun again. Mr. Haverford was gone.

He looked off down the dock. When he saw the group of women in blue, his heart quickened. He leaned over the rail at the side, trying to get a better look, trying to determine whether it was really she or not.

". . . Combat Information Center just behind the door here on your right," a voice said behind him. "Love to take you in there, but security regulations prohibit that, I'm afraid."

He turned rapidly and saw the group of visitors led by Mr. Carlucci. One of the bright-eyed matrons asked, "Is that where they keep the radar?"

"Yes, ma'am," Mr. Carlucci said.

"Couldn't we just . . ."

"I'm sorry, ma'am," Mr. Carlucci said politely. "Security. The ladder up ahead leads to the bridge, and if you'll follow me I'll show you the real brains of the ship."

The matron squealed, and then the guided party went past him and clanked up the ladder to the bridge. He went back to the rail and looked over at the rapidly advancing women in blue. She was one of them, he was sure of that. He studied them until he could pick her out, the one on the end, the one with the loose-hipped walk. He watched the way the sun silhouetted her; even a uniform couldn't hide her figure. He found it difficult to breathe, and he was surprised to find a grin covering his face. She was looking up at the ship now, and he was tempted to wave until he remembered.

He drew back his arm and hurried into the passageway. He ran through to the hatch leading to the boat deck, ran out past the forward stack, past the torpedo tubes amidships, and past the ladder leading to the quarter-deck. He didn't want to climb down right near the OD. He ran past the hanging motor launch, past the aft stack, and then down the ladder aft of the quarter-deck. He reached the main deck as she stepped onto the gangway.

The rifles were snapped back again, and the hands crossed in salute. He saw her raise her own hand in salute, and he thought how ridiculous women in war were, but he shoved the thought aside. She was not just a "woman in war." She was Claire, and she was a nurse.

She stepped onto the quarter-deck now, threw a snappy salute at the ensign flying from the fantail, and then saluted the OD. The OD returned the salute, and she smiled and then waited for the other nurses to catch up with her. He wondered how he could get rid of the others, but she knew he was waiting for her, and she'd help him.

She looked around casually, and he knew she was looking for him, and the thought pleased him. He waited until the other nurses were aboard, six of them, and then watched as the OD assigned them a guide. Claire fell in behind the rest, and as they passed through the midships passageway, she glanced over her shoulder, looking directly at him, but showing no sign of recognition.

A smart girl, he thought. A very smart girl.

He climbed up to the boat deck again, crossed to the starboard side, and saw that they had not come out of the passageway. He figured their first stop would be sick bay, the logical place to show off to visiting nurses. He ran back to the port side, and then into the passageway that led past the radar shack, and then down the ladder leading to the main deck. He kept going down, stopping on the ladder that went below decks to the mess hall. He waited there until he saw them step into the other end of the passageway. The guide showed them sick bay, and they nodded appreciatively and murmured among themselves.

Claire was behind the other nurses, and he couldn't see her too well. He heard the guide say something, and then they started down the passageway, coming toward him. He went a step farther down the ladder so that just the top of his white hat was showing, and then down another step so that he was unseen.

The party went past him and started up the ladder to the bridge. He looked up from where he stood on the ladder and saw a flurry of strong legs and white petticoats. The nurses were chattering excitedly among themselves. They did not hear him when he urgently whispered, "Claire!"

She turned abruptly, saw him standing on the ladder below her, and stopped as the other nurses continued up to the bridge. He climbed the steps rapidly, waited until the rest of the party was gone, and then said, smiling, "Hello, Claire."

"Hello," she said. He thought her voice sounded distant, but he attributed that to their current surroundings. Her hat was perched jauntily on her black curls. Her hair framed her face, and there was a high flush on her cheeks. He wanted to take her in his arms and hold her tight, but he was painfully aware of the officer's emblem on her hat and the gleaming silver bar on her shoulder.

"This way," he said.

He led her up the ladder and stopped in the passageway outside C.I.C.

"This is the radar shack," he said. "No visitors are allowed here."

"Do you think—"

"It's all right, Claire," he said. He fished into the pocket of his jumper and came up with a key. He inserted that in the door lock, looked down the passageway, and then rapidly twisted it and swung the door open in one smooth motion. He took her arm, pulled her inside, and then closed the door and locked it.

The room was dark. The radar gear was not operating, and the only light came from behind one of the plotting boards in the corner.

He turned to her and took her shoulders, drawing her close to him in the darkness.

"I didn't think you'd come," he said.

She pulled away from him gently, but he felt the stiffening of her shoulders, and he wished the room weren't quite so dim, wished that he could see her face more clearly.

"I wasn't going to," she said.

Her voice sounded strange and distant. He saw her reach into her purse, and then a match flared, and he saw the fine planes of her face for just an instant as she lighted her cigarette. The match went out, and there was only the dimness again.

"Why . . . why not?" he asked. He felt his own hands go to his jumper pocket again. He pulled one cigarette free from the package in the pocket, lighted it, and then blew out a wreath of smoke nervously. "Why not, Claire?"

"I've been thinking."

"What about? What about, Claire?"

"Us."

She was silent for a moment. She drew in on her cigarette, and the dull red glow lighted her mouth and the tip of her nose.

"What about us?" he said softly.

"It's no good."

"Why not?" he asked defensively.

"Don't shout. For God's sake, do you want the ship down around our ears?"

"I'm sorry," he said sulkily.

"Look, let's be sensible about all this. You were sent to the hospital on the base, and you met a nurse there. All right, it was all fine and dandy. I don't know why I agreed to see you after you left the hospital, but that was all right, too. We'll forget all that. We'll say it was all right."

"Forget—"

"Let me do the talking, please. Don't make it harder for me than it is."

"But you're talking as if this is a new thing. For God's sake, Claire, we've been seeing each other for a month now. That week end in Wilmington—can you—"

"Let's forget that week end in Wilmington. That was something that never should have happened."

"Never should have—"

"I told you not to shout!"

He was nervous now. His hands were beginning to tremble, and he could feel a sick panic inside him. He felt the way he'd felt that time the Old Man had chewed him out on the bridge. He felt exactly like that. He dropped his butt and stepped on it quickly.

"Are you ready to listen?" she asked.

"Yes. Yes, go on."

"I'm trying to tell you I don't like this sneaking around. You know the regulations as well as I do."

"Regulations! How does that apply to two people in—"

"It applies. It damn well applies, because nursing is my career. I'm not going to get kicked out because of an affair with an enlisted man!"

She almost spat the words out, and they hung in the silence of the compartment, dripping their venom.

"So that's it."

"That's it."

"Look, Claire . . ."

"It's over. Please don't try to—"

"Claire, I'm up for another week end soon. We could go to Wilmington again. The same place, Claire. Claire, nobody even knew we were in the service. We could wear civvies again and—"

"No."

"Claire, you can't just chuck it all overboard like that."

"Why can't I? Why on earth can't I? Damnit, you're all the same. You date a girl a few times, and right off you think you own her."

"A few times? A few times?" He reached for her. "Claire . . ."

"Get away from me," she said. "Please, can't you understand it's no good? Can't you see that?"

He grasped her shoulders viciously and pulled her to him. "No," he said through clenched teeth. "No, I can't see it. I can't see it at all. Claire, baby . . ."

"Oh, for God's sake!" She pulled away and reached for the doorknob, and he clamped his fingers onto her wrist. "Let me go," she said tightly.

"No."

"Look, you don't want me to start yelling, do you? You know what happens when a nurse screams rape, don't you? Now get your hands off me."

He brought his hand up viciously, almost before he realized what he was doing. The open palm collided with her cheek, and there was the dull sound of the slap, and the stinging sensation on his hand.

She backed away from him and brought her hand up slowly to her cheek. "You're dirty," she said. "You're dirty and filthy and common. I must have been out of my mind."

"I'm . . . I'm sorry, Claire. I . . ."

"Get out of my way. Open that door or you'll be chopping rocks in Portsmouth tomorrow."

"Claire, you're just upset. You—"

"Do you want me to start screaming?"

"Claire . . ."

"All right! All right, I warned you." She opened her mouth to scream, and a shock sped through him. He reached out and clamped his hand onto her mouth, feeling it slide slippery with lipstick under his palm. She struggled and then tried to bite his hand. She twisted her head, freeing her mouth for an instant, opening it wide in an attempt to scream again.

He seized her throat, and they struggled across the room, crashing into the Sugar George gear, reeling over to slam against one of the plotting tables. A set of sound-powered phones clattered to the deck, and he thought, What happens if I let her go now?

His hands tightened around the soft flesh of her throat, and he felt the muscles cord in protest, stand out in firm relief against his palms. He kept tightening his hands, and she kicked out at him, one shoe falling from her foot. Her eyes bulged in the dim light on the plotting board, wide, wider, and then she shuddered and he felt the shudder and knew it was all over. She hung limply at the end of his arms, and he dropped her quickly to the deck. Her lighted cigarette rolled away from her body, and he stepped on it quickly, grinding it out under his heel.

He looked down at her. Her skirt had hiked up over her thighs, and he saw the taut ribbing of her stockings, the garters biting into her flesh, and he thought, It could have been different.

He was sweating. He wiped the beaded drops from his upper lip, took a last look around the room, and then crossed the corner, ducking under the plotting board. He listened at the door there, heard nothing, and quickly opened it. The door led to the sonar shack. He could avoid the ladder leading to the bridge this way. The guides wouldn't be showing the sound gear, either. He could duck through the sonar shack and then get down to the main deck. He'd mix with the other men, maybe wander toward the fantail, and drop the key to the radar shack over the side.

Rapidly he closed the door behind him.

Chuck Masters sat upright in his bunk. He was wearing a T-shirt and gray trousers, and his dog tags pressed their imprint against the thin fabric of his shirt. He lighted a cigarette, looked up at the executive officer, and said, "Mike, I'd prefer to be left off the board. Honestly, I'd prefer it."

Mike Reynolds shook his head. "It can't be done, Chuck. I'm short of lieutenants."

"You can swing it if you want to," Masters said petulantly.

"Can't, believe me. The Old Man wants an investigation board. Damnit, you know how many people are involved in this mess?''

"How many?" Masters asked dryly.

"Plenty. First we got the Squadron Commander by blinker light, and then we sent a messenger with a formal note. Then we had to inform SOPA, and then the Commandant of the Fifth Naval District. SOPA sent over a legal officer and an intelligence officer, and now—''

"Are those the two meatheads I saw sticking their fingers into my radar gear?"

"Yes. They don't count, though. The FBI is on its way."

"The FBI?" Chuck whistled softly. "Why them?"

"First, because there were civilians aboard when the nurse got it, and second, because this ship is a federal reservation. If prosecution is ever started, it'll go right to the U.S. Attorney for trial in a federal district court."

"That's just my point. We've got all these people on it already. Those two meatheads, and now the FBI. Why the hell do we need an investigation board of our own?"

Reynolds shook his head. "You just don't know the Navy. The Old Man has three stripes, and he'd like four. If he can crack this himself, it'll be fine. You think a dead nurse in his radar shack helps him get that fourth stripe?"

"I bleed for him," Masters said.

"Bleed for me a little, Chuck," Reynolds put in quickly. "We need the board. The Old Man says five men and a recorder. He wants a senior member, and I'm it. I need three other members and they should be lieutenants, and I need a junior officer and one of the yeomen as recorder."

"So?"

"So I've got Carlucci and Davis as my two lieutenants, and I've got Ensign Le Page—''

"That moron?"

"I need a junior officer. I've got this yeoman second— what the hell's his name?—Schaefer, yeah, and I need one more lieutenant."

"Why the hell pick on me?"

"Can you think of anyone else? This is a tin can, Chuck, not a battle wagon."

"How about Ed?"

"He's on leave. Look, Chuck, I went over the whole list. You're it."

"Is that an order?"

"Order, hell. If you want to put it that way, yes. It's an order. Now get off your dead rump and put a shirt on. We're meeting in the wardroom in ten minutes. The Old Man wants us to get started before the G-men show up."

"Private eyes," Masters said disgustedly.

"What the hell are you kicking about? The FBI'll probably crack this before we even get to ask a question."

"I still wish you'd leave me out of it. I'm in it too much already."

"How so?"

"The broad was found in the radar shack. I'm communications officer."

"Don't be bitter," Reynolds cracked. "Things are bad all over."

Masters thought of that as he walked ashore to the nurses' quarters that afternoon. Things were certainly bad when a respectable communications officer began playing gumshoe. He looked up at the sign that told him he'd reached his destination, sighed heavily, and mounted the low flat steps.

He entered a long wide room scattered with easy chairs and couches. A few women were reading quietly, and one stood near a piano at the end of the room. He walked quickly to the information desk, took off his hat, and waited. The young Wave at the switchboard looked up and smiled.

"Can I help you, sir?" she asked.

"Yes. I'm looking for Miss Dvorak. She's expecting me. I'm on the investigation board of the *Sykes.*"

"Oh," the Wave said. "About Miss Cole?"

"Yes."

She glanced behind her at a large board from which an array of white disks hung. Each disk bore a number, and she consulted these briefly and said, "I believe Miss Dvorak is in, sir. Won't you have a seat?"

"Thank you," he said. He fingered the brim of his hat and then walked self-consciously to one of the easy chairs. He sat, and realized she'd have no place to sit when she came out, so he stood abruptly, feeling foolish, and walked to one of the couches and sat again. A nurse across the room glanced up, and he examined her crossed legs briefly and then turned his head away. The Wave at the switchboard was saying something into the phone, so it couldn't be very long now. He made himself as comfortable as he could, and he waited.

He'd been waiting for about five minutes when she came through the door at the end of the room. She walked rapidly, her crisp white skirt flaring out from good legs. She was blonde, and her cap sat primly on her head, its single gold stripe catching the sun that glanced through the windows. He stood and faced her, and when she saw him, she walked directly to him.

"Miss Dvorak?" he asked.

"Yes, sir," she said. "Mr. Masters?"

He nodded and said, "Sit down, won't you? I hope I didn't pull you away from anything?"

"No, not at all, sir. Please forgive my uniform. I just came off duty."

"That's quite all right," he said, some of her starched formality spreading to him. "I just wanted to ask a few questions about Claire Cole. She was your roommate, wasn't she?"

"Yes, sir."

"She was a lieutenant j.g.?"

"Yes, sir."

"How long did you room together?"

"Since I was assigned to the hospital, sir. Six months."

"I see." He felt awkward, and the girl's attitude wasn't helping him any. Why the hell couldn't she relax? "Er, were you with her on Navy Day? When she went aboard the *Sykes,* I mean?"

"Yes, sir, I was."

"Can you tell me what happened?"

"Well, I can only tell you what happened while she was with us. I mean, I don't know anything about how—about how she was killed."

"I understand."

"Well, we went aboard the *Sykes* at about three—at about fifteen hundred, sir. Claire boarded her first, and waited on the quarter-deck for the rest of us. We went in a group, you see."

"I see."

"The OD assigned a guide to us, a young gunner's mate, I believe, and he took us to sick bay, and then he was taking us up to show us the bridge. That's when Claire disappeared."

"Did you notice her absence at the time?"

"No, sir, I didn't."

"Let's drop the sir stuff, shall we?"

"Yes, si . . ."

She caught herself and smiled, and he marveled at the change that came over her face when she smiled. She looked almost pretty, and he found himself staring at her, and then remembered he was supposed to be questioning her.

"When did you notice she was gone?"

"When we were on the bridge, si . . . when we were on the bridge. I looked around, and Claire wasn't there."

"What did you do then?"

"I went to the ladder and looked down, and I called her name. There was no answer. I figured she'd gone ahead. I mean, Claire was a girl who could take care of herself."

"How do you mean?"

"Well, she could take care of herself."

"With men, do you mean?"

The girl blushed, and Masters was so surprised he almost burst out laughing. "Yes, sir, with men."

"Did she have many boy friends?"

"Yes, sir. I believe she did."

"Any aboard the *Sykes?*"

"Sir?"

"My name is Chuck," he said, "if that'll make it any easier."

"I'm sorry."

"Believe me, I don't like this any more than you do. Let's just try to relax, and maybe we'll get somewhere."

"All right," she said, and then belatedly added, "Chuck."

"That's better. Did she have any boy friends aboard the *Sykes?*"

"I really don't know."

"Did she ever mention the men she dated?"

"Not too often."

"But sometimes?"

"Yes, sometimes. But she never mentioned anyone aboard the *Sykes.*"

"Was it her suggestion to visit the *Sykes* on Navy Day?"

"I don't remember."

"Think."

"I don't know. I think it just sort of came up, you know, one of those things. I don't think any one of us made the suggestion."

"Someone must have made the suggestion," he said, irritated with her answer.

"Do you want me to say she made it?" the girl asked. "Will that help you?"

"I'm sorry," he said. "I guess I'm not very good at playing cop." He paused. "What's your name?"

"Jean."

He smiled. "Nice knowing you."

She seemed uncertain as to what to reply. She smiled briefly and then studied her hands in her lap.

He sighed deeply. "Well, is there anything unusual that might shed some light on this? Anything she said or did?"

"I don't know what's important and what isn't," Jean said.

Masters smiled. "That's exactly my trouble. Perhaps . . . Were there any men she saw regularly?"

"I told you, I really don't know. Unless . . ."

"Unless what?"

"Well," she said, and then stopped. "I don't like to talk about Claire. I mean, I feel strange. She's dead and . . ."

"What is it?"

"Well, about two weeks ago she had a week end, and she was very secretive about where she was going. The girls all kidded her about it, and she kidded them back, but she still wouldn't tell us where she was going."

"What kind of kidding?"

"Oh, you know. The usual. Stuff like 'Be careful, Claire,' stuff like that."

"What did she say?"

Jean blushed again, and Masters waited. "She said . . . Well, really, I . . ."

"What did she say?"

"She said, 'If you're going to do it, do it with a sailor.' "

"Claire said that?"

"Yes."

"I see. Then you think she spent the week end with a sailor?"

"I . . . I guess so. Maybe."

"Did you ever find out where she was going?"

"Yes."

"You did?" he said, enthusiastic now. "Where?"

"Wilmington."

"How do you know?"

"I saw a ticket to Wilmington, Delaware. When she was changing her purse. The ticket was on her dresser."

"One ticket?"

"Yes, just one."

"I see."

"Does it mean anything?"

"It could, I suppose. When was this? Two weeks ago, did you say?"

"Yes."

"I suppose it'd be simple enough to see which of our men had week end passes two weeks ago," he said. Then he rose abruptly and extended his hand. "Thanks a lot, Jean. It was a pleasure meeting you."

She rose, too, taking his hand in a firm, warm grip. "I hope I gave you something you can use," she said. She smiled then, and he marveled again at the transformation.

"Listen," he said. "I know this is a little abrupt, but . . . well, I feel awful about putting you through an inquisition, and I'd like to make up for it. Do you suppose we could have dinner together?"

"Well, I don't know. I . . ."

"A movie on the base, then? How's that? A movie and a soda afterward? I know you haven't got the duty because you just came off. What do you say?"

She looked at him steadily for a few moments. At last she said, "No, sir. I don't think so. Thank you, though."

The smile dropped from Masters' face. "Well, thanks anyway," he said. He felt awkward again, and his fingers roamed the band of his hat. "Thanks," he said once more, and then turned on his heel and walked past the information desk, and down the low steps.

2

WHEN FREDERICK NORTON AND MATTHEW DICKASON stepped off the plane at Norfolk Air Base, there was probably not a man within a radius of three miles who did not know they were FBI agents.

Their appearance was in no way responsible for this widespread knowledge, for they looked like anything but federal men. They did not wear trench coats or low-slung fedoras. Their artillery did not form conspicuous bulges under their jackets. They did not move furtively, nor did they steal about with catlike treads.

Frederick Norton was a somewhat portly man of about forty-five, wearing a gray pin-stripe suit and a neat gray Homburg. His white-on-white shirt was clipped securely at the collar with a slender gold pin. He wore a narrow blue silk tie upon which a gold fleur-de-lis design had been skillfully embroidered. He looked like a tired businessman whose plane had accidentally put down in Norfolk rather than the Palm Beach for which it was bound. Even his jowly cheeks and cold eyes bore out the simile.

Matthew Dickason might have been Norton's office boy. He wore a rumpled brown tweed suit and no hat. His hair was clipped close to his head, in the fashion he'd affected all through college and law school. He had clear blue eyes and a slightly pug nose, and though he was pushing thirty, he could have passed for a college freshman, and often did.

The two men stepped from the plane and into a waiting jeep, and every pilot and crewman within viewing distance knew that these were the two G-men who were com-

ing to clear up the mess about the dead nurse. The jeep
contained a coxswain and a full lieutenant. The full lieutenant shook hands with the two agents, snapped a terse
order at the coxswain, and then leaned back as the jeep
crossed the airfield and headed for the naval base.

"Have you ever been in Norfolk before?" the lieutenant
asked Norton.

"No," Norton said.

"A nice little town," the lieutenant ventured. "You'll
like it."

"Will I?" Norton said.

"Well, yes. Yes, I think you will."

"I'm glad," Norton said. He reached into his inside
jacket pocket and took out a leather cigar case. He carefully removed and unwrapped one cigar. From his vest
pocket he extracted a small pair of silver scissors, with
which he promptly snipped off the end of the cigar. He
did not offer one to Dickason because he knew Dickason
did not smoke. He did not offer one to the lieutenant because he knew their relationship would be terminated as
soon as the jeep reached the ship. He was sure as hell not
going to waste a good cigar on someone he'd never see
again. He lighted the cigar and relaxed, watching the scenery of the base unfold as the jeep bounced its way through
the clean, well-ordered streets.

"Yes," the lieutenant said, "I think you'll enjoy your
stay here."

Norton puffed on his cigar and said nothing.

"Much to do in town?" Dickason asked. His voice, in
contrast with his boyish appearance, was rather deep and
full chested.

"Well, there's always something to do," the lieutenant
said, "if you know where to look."

"And you know where to look, is that it?" Norton
asked.

The lieutenant smiled graciously. "I've been stationed
here for three years now," he said.

"You deserve the Navy Cross," Norton answered.

The lieutenant didn't know quite what to answer to that one. He blinked at Norton for a moment, and then retreated in silence for the remainder of the ride. The U.S.S. *Sykes* was not a bad-looking ship. It had long clean lines, and it bristled with guns. The man in the street, who couldn't tell a cruiser from a PT boat, would probably have considered the *Sykes* a superdreadnaught battleship. It was not a battleship. It was a destroyer, and the name was an aptly chosen one, with its connotations of great destructive power. The jeep pulled up to the gangway, and the lieutenant shook hands with Dickason and Norton before leaving them there.

"Well," Dickason said, "here's the boat."

"The ship," Norton corrected. "If these Navy morons hear you calling it a boat, they'll keelhaul you."

He puffed on his cigar and studied the low-slung litheness of the ship. He cleared his throat, then snorted, flipped his cigar butt into the water, and walked up the gangway. Dickason followed close behind him. A crowd of sailors had already gathered at the rails. Norton ignored the crowd. He walked with his head down, watching the wood of the gangway. He did not lift his head until he was standing on the quarter-deck, and then his eyes looked into the smiling cherub face that belonged to Ensign Le Page.

Le Page extended a chubby, freckled hand.

"Mr. Norton?" he asked. "Mr. Dickason?"

"Yes," Norton said briefly.

"I'm Ensign Le Page, officer of the deck."

"How do you do?" Norton said.

"The captain is expecting you, gentlemen. I'll tell him you're here."

"Thank you."

Le Page picked up a hand phone resting on the platform amidships. He said something into the phone and then turned to face the two agents.

"He'll see you now. He's in the wardroom." Le Page snapped his fingers at the gunner's mate who was standing watch with him as messenger. "Take these gentlemen to the wardroom," he said.

The gunner's mate nodded and began walking forward. Norton snorted and followed him, aware of the inquisitive eyes on him. Dickason looked up at the stack, and then at the mast, and then at the bridge, like a sight-seer in New York City. The messenger took them into a passageway and knocked on a door.

"Yes?"

"OD asked me to bring these men to you, Captain," the gunner's mate said.

"Show them in," Commander Glenburne said from behind the closed door.

The gunner's mate opened the door and then stood at attention while Norton and Dickason stepped inside. He closed the door behind them, and Glenburne rose and extended a tanned hand. He was a man of about fifty-two, tall and lean, with a complexion burned brown from years of standing on an open bridge. His grip was firm, and Norton had never liked these manly characters with the too-firm grips.

"Gentlemen," Glenburne said, "glad you arrived. Have a seat, won't you?"

Norton and Dickason made themselves comfortable at the long table.

"Coffee?" Glenburne asked.

Dickason seemed ready to say, "Yes," but Norton replied, "No," for both of them.

"Have a nice trip?" Glenburne asked.

"We came by plane," Norton answered.

"One of our Navy planes, eh? Got to hand it to—"

"The Army brought us," Norton said.

"Oh." Glenburne cleared his throat. "Well, I suppose we'd better get right down to business. You know all about the dead nurse, I suppose."

"Yes," Norton said.

"Hell of a thing. Haven't got enough worries, they have

to leave a corpse in my radar shack." Glenburne shook his head. "Well, you boys will clear all that up."

"Yes," Norton said.

"I've already appointed an investigation board." Glenburne smiled. "Figured we'd snoop around and see what—"

"Have you restricted all your men to the ship?" Norton asked.

"Why, no. I mean, that is, it never occurred to me. Do you suppose—"

"If one of them is a murderer, it might be a good idea," Norton said dryly.

"Yes. Yes, of course. I'll—I'll do that. I'll have that done at once." The Captain walked to a phone and connected himself with the quarter-deck. "Le Page, get me the Executive Officer. Send him to the wardroom. Get me Masters, too, will you?" He listened for a moment, and then replaced the phone. "Masters is my communications officer. He'll take you to the radar shack, show you where the girl was found. I imagine you'll want to get started right away."

"Yes," Norton said.

"I'll ask Mike . . . Reynolds, my executive officer, to restrict the men to the ship. I'm certainly glad you gentlemen are here. My investigation board hasn't—"

"Captain," Norton said, "I hope this board of yours isn't going to get underfoot."

"What?" Glenburne asked.

"Your investigation board. A lot of amateurs dickering in murder are liable to screw up the works. Do you understand, sir?"

"Well, yes. But . . ."

"You can have your board, if you like. Please don't misunderstand me. I sincerely hope, though, that they'll confine their investigation to—"

"I had hoped they could be of assistance. After all—"

"*Con*-fine their investigation," Norton said over Glenburne's voice, "to a compilation of the facts for the ship's record. In other words, we'll welcome evidence, but we don't want them working at cross purposes with us."

"I see."

A discreet knock sounded on the wardroom door.

"Come in," Glenburne said harshly.

Mike Reynolds opened the door and stepped into the room. "You sent for me, Captain?" he said.

"Yes. I want you to restrict all the men to the ship, starting at once. Cancel liberty for all watch sections."

"Yes, sir," Reynolds said.

"Captain," Norton said.

"Yes?"

"That order includes officers, too, I hope."

"Officers?"

"I assumed that 'men,' in Navy jargon means 'enlisted men.' I want the officers restricted, too."

"But surely you don't think—"

"Captain, until I know better, even *you* may have killed that nurse."

"I see." Glenburne forced a smile that didn't quite come off. "All right, Mike," he said. "Restrict all officers and men to the ship." He turned to Norton. "I hope this will not include my investigation board."

Norton shrugged. "All right, give your board free rein."

"Thank you. Take care of that, will you Mike?"

"Yes, sir." Reynolds walked to the door and opened it, catching Masters in the act of raising his fist to knock. Glenburne spotted Masters and said, "Come in, Chuck, come in." Masters stood to one side while Reynolds stepped into the passageway. He winked at Reynolds and then went into the wardroom, closing the door behind him.

"Chuck," Glenburne said, "Mr. Norton and Mr. Dickason, the FBI men we've been expecting. Gentlemen, this is Mr. Masters, my communications officer." Glenburne cleared his throat. "He is also a member of the investigation board."

Norton took Masters' hand. "How do you do?"

Masters returned the grip, and then shook hands with Dickason. "Gentlemen," he said.

"I told these gentlemen you'd show them the radar shack, Chuck. You can do that right now, if you like. That is, I have nothing further to say." The Old Man looked miffed, and Masters wondered what had happened before he'd arrived.

"Yes, sir," he said. "If you'll come with me, gentle—"

"Oh, yes," Glenburne said, "one other thing. If you'd like, I can find quarters for you on the ship. I'm sure some of my officers wouldn't mind—"

"We'll stay in town, thank you," Norton said.

"I see." Glenburne cleared his throat. "Well, good luck."

"Thank you," Norton said. He followed Masters and Dickason out of the wardroom and into the passageway.

"Right up this ladder," Masters said over his shoulder. The FBI men followed soundlessly. When they were in the passageway outside C.I.C., Masters said, "This is the radar shack. We've kept it locked since the day of the murder."

"The body's been removed, hasn't it?"

"Yes. But we chalked the deck for you. So you'll know where she was lying. We haven't touched anything in here."

"Except the doorknob," Norton said dryly.

"Sir?"

"You've got your hand all over it right this minute," Norton said. "How many other people have smeared the prints that might have been on that knob?"

Masters drew his hand back suddenly, as if the brass knob had magically grown hot. "I'm sorry. I didn't think."

"Is the door locked?" Norton asked.

"Yes, sir."

"Has it been locked since the day of the murder?"

"Yes, sir."

"Was it locked when you discovered the body?"

"Yes, sir."

"All right, open it. What's down the hallway there?"

"The radio shack, sir," Masters said. "And beyond that, the boat deck. Through the hatch there."

"All right, open the door."

Masters unlocked the door and swung it wide. The room was in absolute darkness.

"Were there any lights on when you found the body?" Norton asked.

"Only on one of the plotting boards," Masters said. "The overhead lights were off."

"Mmmm." Norton looked around. "Where's the light switch?"

"On your left, sir."

Norton flashed a handkerchief out of his breast pocket, opened it over his fingers, and turned the lights on. The radar gear was lined up on the bulkhead to his right. The plotting tables were opposite the gear, with a vertical plotting board diagonally in front of the door leading to the sound shack. Norton looked around the room silently.

"This where you found the body?" Dickason asked, indicating the chalked outline on the deck.

"Yes, sir."

"She was strangled, that right?"

"Yes, sir."

"We'll have to check that, Fred," Dickason said. "May be prints on her throat."

"May be," Norton said pessimistically. "Those cigarettes there when you found her?"

"Yes, sir."

Norton stooped and picked the cigarettes up with his handkerchief, carefully folding the linen around them. "Anyone touch these?"

"No, sir."

"Where's the girl's body now?"

"At the base hospital, I believe," Masters said. "They were holding it for you, I think. The girl's parents—"

"All right, we'll take a look later," Norton said. "You can go now, Mr. Masters."

Masters hesitated, and then said, "I questioned the girl's roommate. She told me—"

"What's her name, Mr. Masters?"

"Jean Dvorak."

"Where can we find her?"

"She's a nurse here on the base. You can—"

"Thank you. We'll get to her later."

"She told me—"

"We'll get to her later," Norton said.

Masters nodded blankly. "Well, if you need me . . ."

"We'll ask the Captain for you. Thanks again for your assistance, Mr. Masters."

Masters nodded again and walked to the door. He hesitated, looked back into the room, and then left.

"An investigation board!" Norton said sourly.

Dickason shrugged. "They may turn up something, Fred. You never can tell."

"You're new at this business," Norton said. "Take it from me, boy, they won't turn up a damned thing. I've had experience with this kind of setup before."

"A Navy ship, you mean?"

"No, but a similar setup. An American Legion post once. Entertainer killed there. We got in on the act because the girl had come over the state line. The veterans worked up what they called an investigating committee. Goddamnit, I wanted to shoot them all before I finally got off it."

"Well, these guys—"

"These guys are all laymen. Like the doorknob. We *might* have got something from it. Now all we've got is a record of every slob who entered this room since the nurse got it. Oh, hell."

"Think we'll get anything from the cigarettes?"

"I don't know. We'd better send those to Washington for a real run-through. I think you'd better dust this room to see what else you can pick up."

"What are you going to do, Fred?"

"I want to take a look at the body. And then I'll question this nurse. Maybe she knows something."

"That officer said—"

"Yes, I know. He's already questioned her. He's probably confused her so that she'll be worthless now. Why the hell can't people leave technical jobs to technicians? Suppose I came in and started screwing around with his radar? Christ, he'd blow his top."

Dickason began laughing suddenly.

"What's so funny?" Norton asked.

"The Captain. You really laid down the law with him."

"I had to. Look at it this way, Matt: He's the captain of this ship, used to bossing around everybody he runs into. All right, if I didn't let him know where he stood, he'd think we were a couple more of his lackeys. He may be the boss here normally, but during the run of this investigation, we're in charge. I wanted him to know that from go."

"You really think the old guy might have killed her?"

Norton shrugged. "He doesn't look as if he'd touch a fly." He paused. "Unless it were unzipped."

"Yok-yok," Dickason said.

"Go down and get your gear," Norton said. "You'd better get started here as soon as possible."

"While you look at the stiff."

"While I look at the stiff. Want to come along?"

"No, thanks."

"I figured. They should have grown a beard on you and sent you to Russia, Matt. That's the work for you. Cloak and dagger."

"Up yours," Dickason said.

Norton snorted and stamped out of the radar shack.

3

"YOU'RE JUST ASSUMING IT WAS AN ENLISTED MAN," THE exec said to Masters. "That's officer prejudice."

"No, sir, it is not," Masters said. "It is nothing of the sort. It is sheer calculation, worthy of Sherlock Holmes himself. I'm wasting my time in this goddamned Navy, that's all."

"All right, Sherlock, let me hear it."

"Right. I figured it was an officer at first because I couldn't think of any way for an enlisted man to meet a nurse socially. They don't go to dances together, and they usually don't frequent the same dives. So it had to be an officer. Assuming, of course, that whoever killed Claire Cole knew her."

"Go on."

"All right, so this Dvorak girl tells me Claire went on a Wilmington week end with somebody. Two weeks ago. I checked the ship's list. Three officers went off that week end."

"And who were they?"

"Carlucci. He went to New York to see his wife. Haverford. He went to Norfolk, and you know what he did there. He came back stinking blind. I know he left the ship with thirty dollars and with no change of clothing. He sure as hell wasn't preparing for a week end in Wilmington. Besides, I saw him in Norfolk that Sunday."

"So who was the third officer?"

"You, Mike."

"I'll be damned," Reynolds said.

"So the officer assumption is out. Unless you killed her."

"Don't be silly," Reynolds said, a little miffed.

"I didn't think you did, Mike. So I started looking over the list of enlisted men who had that week end."

"There must have been plenty."

"There were. The entire second-watch section."

Reynolds pulled a face. "That narrowed it down considerably, didn't it?"

"Hardly. Something else did, though."

"What?"

"Claire Cole was killed in the radar shack. On Navy Day, the shack was locked. That meant whoever killed her had a key."

"We've already gone through every man's locker," Reynolds said. "If you think—"

"I'm not saying he still has it, Mike. But he had it in order to get into the shack. That's for sure."

"All right, go on."

"I asked myself who among the enlisted men would possess a key to the radar shack."

"Who indeed?" Reynolds asked.

"A radarman, of course. That was my first thought. You know the radar bunch. They're always in there making coffee and what the hell, and if one has a key, they all have it. But someone else could get a key, too."

"Who?"

"A yeoman."

"I don't follow."

"There are keys to every room and compartment on this ship in the yeoman's office."

"The key to the radar shack is still there," Reynolds said.

"Sure, but that doesn't mean anything. If whoever killed her was planning on having her aboard, he'd also plan on where to take her when she was aboard. He could have had a duplicate key made from the one in the yeoman's office."

"All right, I'll grant you that. So it could have been either a radarman or a yeoman. How many of each went on liberty that week end?"

"Six radarmen and three yeomen."

"That really does narrow it down."

"Considerably. And I've narrowed it down even further."

"How?"

"Well, I wondered how an enlisted man could meet a nurse, and get to know her well enough to propose a week end in Wilmington. The answer was simple."

Reynolds sighed heavily. "What was the answer?"

"He was in the hospital."

Reynolds' eyes narrowed in interest. "Go on, Chuck," he said.

"I checked, Mike. Since we pulled into the base, thirty men have been to the hospital. Twelve were there within the last three months, and of those, eleven were there for a week or more. Of the eleven, eight were on Claire Cole's ward."

"So?"

"Two of those eight men were radarmen. Three were yeomen."

"Seems to indicate a high sick rate among the white-collar ratings, doesn't it? What else did you find?"

"I carried it all the way down, Mike. Of the two radarmen, one had liberty on that week end Claire spent in Wilmington. Of the yeomen, two had liberty then."

"So what have you got now?"

"Names. Three names. Each of the three men had an opportunity to meet and know Claire Cole. Each of the three had week end liberty when she did. And each of the three had access to a radar-shack key."

"And who are they?"

"Alfred Jones, radarman third class; Perry Daniels, yeoman second class; and Richard Schaefer, yeoman second class—the recorder on your investigation board."

Reynolds considered this for a moment. Then he said, "One thing, Chuck."

"What's that?"

"I think the FBI already knows all this."

"Go to hell," Masters said.

He looks honest enough, Masters thought. He certainly doesn't look like a killer.

He studied the thin boy standing before the table in the wardroom. He was tall, with penetrating blue eyes and an angular face. He had large hands, and he clenched and unclenched them nervously now.

"Your name is Alfred Jones?" Masters asked.

"Yes, sir. You know me, sir. I'm in the radar gang."

"Rank?" Masters asked, ignoring Jones's comment.

"Radarman third, sir. Sir, the G-men have already questioned me. I mean, if it's about—"

"At ease, Jones."

Masters looked at the boy and then across the room to where Schaefer, the board recorder, was busily taking notes. "Sit down, Jones," he said. He waved his hand at a chair, and Jones sat in it. He sat on the edge of the seat, Masters noticed. Quickly Masters dipped into the pocket of his shirt, pulled out a pack of cigarettes, and extended it to Jones.

"Smoke?"

Jones shook his head, and his eyes narrowed. "Are you trying to find out whether or not I smoke, sir?"

He surprised Masters. Masters kept his hand out, and he said slowly, "Yes, I am."

"I figured. They found two dead butts in the radar shack, didn't they? One belonged to the broad and one to the guy who strangled her."

"You're well informed, Jones."

Jones shrugged. "Scuttlebutt, sir. I also heard the G-men couldn't find anything but smeared prints on the guy's cigarette." He paused and smiled. "I smoke, sir."

"Have one," Masters said.

"No, thanks."

Masters returned the package to his pocket. "Do you know why you're here, Jones?"

"Sure. I'm a radarman. You figure since the radar shack was locked on Navy Day, it had to be a radarman who opened it. I'm way ahead of you, sir."

"Do you have a key to the radar shack, Jones?"

"I had one."

"What'd you do with it?"

"The same thing every other guy in the radar gang did the minute the nurse turned up. I deep-sixed it."

"Why?"

"Pardon me, sir, but how long have you been in the Navy? I tossed it over the side because all the guys were doing it. I wasn't going to be the only one caught with a key."

"I see."

There was a moment's silence, and Masters glanced across the room at Schaefer. The yeoman's head was bent over his pad, and his pencil worked furiously.

"Are we going too fast for you, Schaefer?" Masters asked.

Schaefer looked up. He had a wide face, expressionless now, with large brown eyes that looked moist. "No, sir."

Masters nodded and turned back to the radarman. "Did you know Claire Cole, Jones?"

"No, sir. I never seen her ever. Not dead or alive."

"Where's Wilmington, Jones?"

"Sir?"

"Where's Wilmington?"

"In Delaware, I guess, ain't it?"

"You ever been there?"

"No, sir."

"When was your last week end liberty, Jones?"

"A couple of weeks ago."

"When exactly?"

"I don't remember the date, sir. It was a few weeks back. Two weeks ago, I think."

"Where'd you go, Jones?"

"Newport News."

"Where in Newport News?"

"One of the flea bags. I don't remember."

"Were you with anyone?"

"Part of the time."

"Who?"

Jones smiled. "You're getting personal, sir."

"Don't get snotty, Jones. Who were you with?"

"Some broad. I picked her up in a bar."

"What was her name?"

"Who knows?"

"When were you with her?"

"Saturday night."

"Think you can find her again?"

"Maybe. Why? What's so important?"

"You sure you don't remember what her name was, Jones?"

"All right, I remember. Agnes. All right?"

"Agnes what?"

"I don't know. You want to know what kind of birthmarks she had on her—"

"That'll be all, Jones."

Jones stood up sullenly. "You don't think I killed that nurse, do you? You don't think that."

"Shove off, Jones," Masters said.

Jones seemed undecided. He wavered for a moment and then said, "I don't feel like no railroad, sir. You get a bunch of brass together and pick on an enlisted man, and I'll be making small ones out of big ones. I never saw that goddamned nurse, and I—"

"Get out, Jones," Masters said, "before you really get into trouble."

Jones snapped to attention, did an abrupt about-face, and headed for the door.

When he was gone, Masters turned to Schaefer and said, "What do you think, boy?"

"About what, sir?"

"This character who was just in here. Was he telling the truth?"

"I wouldn't know, sir," Schaefer said slowly.

"Do you remember Claire Cole, Schaefer?"

"Sir?"

"You were at the base hospital, weren't you?"

"Oh. Oh, yes, sir."

"Do you remember seeing her?"

"Yes, sir," Schaefer said. "Yes, I do."

"Pretty?"

"Yes, sir."

"Would a man remember her if he'd seen her?"

"I—I suppose so, sir."

"Then why do you suppose Jones said he never saw her? Dead or alive. He was on Claire Cole's ward, too."

Schaefer said nothing.

"Why do you suppose, Schaefer?"

"Perhaps he's frightened, sir."

"Are you frightened, Schaefer?"

Schaefer hesitated a long time before answering. Finally he said, "Why should I be, Mr. Masters?"

In the wardroom that evening, after the Old Man had gone up to his cabin, Reynolds and Masters shared a pot of coffee. Reynolds held his steaming white mug in his browned hands, and the vapor framed his face, giving him an evil, satanic look. Masters looked at the exec through the rising steam and said, "You look like hell."

"What?"

"Nothing. A private pun."

"Did you see the Old Man?" Reynolds asked suddenly.

"I saw."

"Brother, don't cross his path, that's all. He could sear the paint off a gun turret, the way he feels."

"Tough," Masters said. "Why the hell doesn't he leave it all to the FBI, the way he's supposed to?"

"He is. But he's still getting chewed out. Homicide on a Navy ship. Hell, it's like the chain of command in reverse. The dead broad's family and friends write letters and send wires to their Congressmen. The Congressmen read them and then begin pressuring BuPers. BuPers hops on its white horse and starts riding CinCLant. CinCLant turns the screws on the squadron commander, and that old bastard jumps on the Old Man, wanting to know why and what for. Now the Old Man has a hair across, and if the FBI or somebody doesn't find out who killed that nurse, this ship is going to resemble nothing in the Atlantic Fleet, brother. I can't blame the Old Man. They're acting as if *he* killed the goddamn broad."

"Maybe he did," Masters said.

"Maybe a flippant attitude is unbecoming," Reynolds said.

"Oh, relax, Mike. What the hell are we supposed to do? We're sailors, not policemen!"

"The nurse was killed on this ship. Everyone is making it the Old Man's headache."

"Sure. Except it's *our* headache."

"How'd you make out with Jones?"

"He's a snotty bastard, you know? As soon as this is over, I'm going to ride him hard."

"Unless he's the murderer."

"If he's the murderer," Masters said, "he's beyond riding."

"You talk to Daniels or Schaefer yet?"

"I'll talk to Daniels in the morning. I'm saving Schaefer."

"Why?"

"First of all, he knows all the questions I'm going to ask. He's our recorder, remember?"

"And second of all?"

"That's all. Just first of all."

Masters found Perry Daniels in the aft sleeping compartment the next morning after sweep-down. The yeoman was sitting on a foot locker, polishing his shoes. A cigarette dangled from the corner of his mouth, and the smoke trailed up past the short-cropped hair on his head. Masters stood at the top of the ladder and studied the man for a few moments. Daniels was twenty-six or so, narrow-boned, with tough sinew covering those bones. He worked the brush over his shoes, and the muscles of his arm rippled with the movement. His eyes were squinted against the rising smoke of the cigarette, and his dog tags rattled as he worked.

Masters cleared his throat and started down into the compartment. There was the sweaty odor of cramped living in the compartment, and Masters wondered if it had been a good idea to come here to talk to the man. Well, it was too late now.

"Daniels?" he asked.

The yeoman looked up, still squinting past the smoke from his cigarette. He put down the brush, plucked the cigarette from his lips, and dropped it to the deck. He was barefoot, so he did not step on it.

"Yes, sir," he said.

He made a motion to rise, and Masters said, "At ease."

With his hand inside one shoe, Daniels reached down for the glowing butt on the deck, brushing it beneath the heel of the shoe.

"I want to ask you a few questions, Daniels," Masters said.

"Certainly, sir." Daniels seemed completely at ease, but Masters wondered if that weren't just a pose. The yeoman unwrapped a polishing cloth, slipped one shoe onto a bare foot, and proceeded to polish it.

"Were you ever confined to the hospital ashore, Daniels?"

"Yes, sir."

"Do you remember a nurse named Claire Cole?"

"Yes, sir. She was the one got killed in the radar shack."

Masters sat down on the locker opposite Daniels. Daniels spat onto the top of his shoe and began working the cloth in earnest, giving the shoe a high gleam.

"You knew her at the hospital?" Masters asked.

"Yes, sir. To talk to. She was very pleasant. Always a cheerful word. A nice girl." Daniels slipped the remain-

ing shoe onto his other foot, spat on it, and got to work
with the cloth again.

"Did you ever try to date her?"

Daniels' eyes opened wide. "Me, sir?"

"Yes, you. Why not?"

"Hell, sir, she was a j.g. I mean, you know."

"What? What do I know?"

"Well, sir, that's fraternization. That ain't allowed."

Daniels' voice held a combination of awe and solemn
respect for authority, and Masters wondered if such naïve
innocence weren't affected. The squawk box on the bulkhead suddenly cleared its throat, and Masters grimaced.
He heard the bosun's whistle, and then a raucous voice
announced, "Now hear this. Now hear this. All hands air
your bedding. All hands air your bedding."

Masters cursed silently. That meant there'd be a rush
into the compartment. Daniels was standing already, stepping out of the shoes and reaching into his locker for a
pair of regulation black socks. He pulled the socks on
quickly, laced the shoes, and then put his shine kit back
into the locker.

"Forget your bedding," Masters said to him. "Come
on topside before the rest of the men come down."

"I want to get a spot up there, sir," Daniels said. "If
I don't take my bedding up now—"

"I'll find a spot for you, Daniels. Later. Come on."

"All right, sir," Daniels said doubtfully.

They climbed the ladder together and Masters walked
to the twin five-inch mount forward of the fantail. He
leaned against the mount and looked out over the water.
Daniels stood beside him, breathing softly.

"You married, Daniels?"

Daniels hesitated a moment. "Sir?"

"Are you married?"

"No, sir. No, I'm not."

"Got a girl?"

"No, sir," he said quickly.

"What'd you think of this Cole dame?"

"Sir?"

"Climb off it, Daniels. Man to man, what'd you think of her?"

"Well, sir, I really . . ."

"Forget my bars, Daniels. What'd you think of Claire Cole?"

Daniels grinned briefly. "I wouldn't kick her out of bed, sir."

"Where'd you go on your week end, Daniels?"

"Norfolk, sir."

"Why that rat town?"

"I was broke, sir."

"Did you see anyone in town?"

"Few of the boys, I guess. I don't really remember."

"Were you alone, then?"

"Yes, sir." Daniels paused. "I like to operate alone, sir. A sailor wolf pack don't get no place."

"Who were the boys you saw in town?"

"I don't remember, sir."

"You didn't go to Wilmington?"

"Sir?"

"Wilmington. Did you go there on your week end?"

"Where's that, sir?"

The men were coming topside with their mattresses now, cursing or laughing or joking. Masters watched them as they plopped their bedding down on top of the depth charges, over the rails, on ammo boxes, everywhere. Daniels shifted uneasily.

"I suppose you can go now, Daniels," Masters said.

"Thank you, sir. It's just I want to find a spot for my bedding, that's all."

"If you have any trouble, look for me, Daniels. I'll make a spot for you."

"Yes, sir, thank you, sir."

"By the way, Daniels. It's Delaware."

Daniels blinked his eyes. *"What's* Delaware, sir?"

"Never mind," Masters said.

4

THE TOWN WAS A NICE TOWN, QUIET AND SEDATE, A SMALL town that somehow managed to escape the temporary look of most small towns. It was a good time of the year for the town, too, the middle of autumn, with leaves shuffling aimlessly underfoot, with winter not yet giving the streets a deserted look and feel.

"This is nice," Dickason said. He walked with a quick spring in his step, matching his strides to Norton's. The weather was uncommonly mild, and Dickason felt as if he were back in college again. He found himself watching the skirts and legs of the girls passing by. He felt good. He felt as if he were doing something. This was a hell of a lot better than dusting for prints in a stuffy radar shack. Shack! Why did they call something made of metal a shack? The Navy. Dickason shook his head. "This is real nice," he said.

"There's only one thing nice about it, Matt."

"What?" Dickason asked.

"It's closer to Washington. It won't cost me as much to phone my wife."

"What made you go into the FBI?" Dickason asked suddenly.

"I like to live dangerously."

"No, seriously."

"Security, salary. How the hell do I know?"

"I know why I went into it."

"Why's that?" Norton asked uninterestedly.

"Days like today. I mean, what we're doing right now. I find this very exciting."

"That's because you're still wet behind the ears. When

you've been in the game a while, you'll begin to hate leg-work.''

"I don't think I could ever hate something like this."

Norton said nothing. The two men walked in silence for a few minutes, and then Dickason asked, "Do you think we'll turn up anything?"

"Maybe," Norton said. "It doesn't matter, anyway."

"Huh?"

"We've narrowed it down to three," Norton said. "All right, we waste today going around with pictures of the dead nurse and the three suspects. Maybe someone will recognize them. Frankly, I doubt it."

"She was a very pretty girl," Dickason said, a little wistfully.

"There are pretty girls everywhere you go. Don't let that fallacy get you, too."

"What fallacy?"

"That a pretty girl will be remembered more than a plain girl will. The human memory is a funny thing. I once had a case where we were able to identify a suspect because a woman remembered a hairy wart on his nose."

"You've had a lot of cases, haven't you, Fred?"

Norton stopped walking. "You know, Matt, sometimes you sound plain stupid," he said.

"What do you mean? Just because I—"

"Skip it, skip it. Yes, I've had a lot of cases. Did I ever tell you about the time I foiled a plot to blow up the Pentagon?"

"Did you really?" Dickason asked.

"Sure. They wanted to fire Hoover after that and give me his job. I wouldn't take it. I'm a very simple man at heart."

"Agh, you're full of crap," Dickason said.

"I know. Come on, here's the next rooming house."

The two men paused before a white clapboard house. The house was small, with twin gables and dormer windows hugging the upper story. Red shutters decorated each window, and a big silver maple in the front yard fought valiantly and fruitlessly to retain its last few browned leaves.

Norton opened the gate and walked to the front stoop. He pulled the old-fashioned bellpull, and then waited.

"What do you think this one'll be?" he asked Dickason.

"I don't understand."

"The expression. When we say we're from the Federal Bureau of Investigation. Shock? Fear? Dead faint? Haven't you ever noticed how the expressions vary?"

"Yes, now that you mention it."

"She'll be an old lady this time," Norton guessed. "When we tell her we're FBI men, she'll invite us in and then give us a list of neighbors she suspects of being Communists."

"I say a young blonde with good legs," Dickason said, joining in the game. It was times like this that made working with Norton a lot of fun.

"I've been doing this for sixteen years now," Norton said, "and I've never had a young blonde with good legs."

The door opened a crack, and a middle-aged woman looked out. She studied Norton's face for a moment before she spoke.

"Yes?" she asked.

"Federal Bureau of Investigation, ma'am," Norton said. "We'd like to ask you a few questions."

They both held out their FBI identification cards.

The woman's hand went involuntarily to her throat. "Oh," she said. "Oh, yes."

"May we come in?"

"Yes, Yes, please do. Is anything wrong? Is something the matter?"

"No, ma'am, just a few routine questions."

"Oh, yes," the woman said. "Come in. Please."

She opened the door wide, and Norton and Dickason stepped into a dim, cool foyer.

"You rent rooms, is that right?" Norton asked.

"Yes, sir. But I have a respectable clientele."

"No question about that, ma'am. We were just wondering if you could identify some photographs for us. If you could tell us whether or not you rented rooms to any of these people."

"Well, I don't know. I mean . . ."

"Suppose you try, ma'am," Norton said. He reached into his jacket pocket for the leather case containing the photographs. He handed the landlady a picture of Claire Cole first. It was a snapshot taken during the summer, with Claire in uniform, a smile on her face, before the nurse's quarters.

"No," the landlady said instantly. "I don't rent to servicewomen."

"Why not?"

"Woman's got no business in the service," she said. "Gallivanting off and fooling around with men. No, I don't rent to servicewomen."

"This girl was a nurse," Norton said.

"Well, I still didn't rent her a room."

"Look at her face," Norton said. "She may have been wearing civilian clothing, so forget the uniform. Did you ever see her before?"

The landlady studied the photograph intently. "No," she said, "never."

"She may have taken a room with a man, and they probably registered as man and wife. Do you recognize any of these pictures?" He handed her photographs of Jones, Schaefer, and Daniels.

"Sailors," the landlady said. "Heavens, no!"

"You don't rent to service*men,* either?" Norton asked.

"Soldiers, yes. But not sailors. Not that drunken lot. Oh, no. I've never had a sailor in my home, and I never will have."

"As I said," Norton told her, "they may have been in civilian clothing. Would you study their faces again, please?"

The landlady looked at the pictures, examining each one carefully. "No, I've never seen any of these people before. Not the girl, and not the men either. Why? They do something?"

"Thank you, ma'am," Norton said. "Sorry to have troubled you."

"They do something?" the landlady asked again.

Norton was already outside on the stoop. Dickason turned and waved. " 'By,'' he said cheerily.

They walked together to the gate, Norton silent.

"She was a bitch, wasn't she?'' Dickason said.

"Not particularly.''

"I mean—''

"Because she's choosy about who lives under her roof? That's her prerogative. I don't much go for sailors, either.''

"Well,'' Dickason said.

"This is all going to be a waste of time anyway,'' Norton said. "Where the hell's that damn list again?'' He reached into his pocket and came up with a letter on an FBI letterhead. He ran down the list, selected one of the addresses, and penciled it out. "That takes care of that one. About seven more to go. You feel up to it, or you want to stop for some coffee first?''

"I could use some coffee,'' Dickason said.

"You're beginning to catch on,'' Norton answered, smiling.

"Why do you think this is going to be a waste of time, Fred?''

"It is,'' Norton said.

"But why?''

"Because I don't think anyone will remember them. Besides, this will all work out fine, anyway. We'll be in Washington before you know it.''

"How so?''

"Look at it this way, Matt: There's a murderer somewhere aboard that ship. We figure he's one of three men, or at least the circumstantial evidence—as slim as it is— points to one of these three men. We couldn't possibly get a conviction on what we've got now, but our murderer doesn't know that. Unless he's supersmart.''

"Maybe he is,'' Dickason said.

"A supersmart murderer doesn't kill in his own back yard. So I figure this pigeon isn't too clever.''

"All right, so what?''

"So he's not too smart. He's been in the Navy for a

while, and he's scared stiff of authority. He's killed an officer, and that officer was a woman, and he knows damn well he's in hot water. There's a big hubbub aboard ship, and on the base, and in the fleet. He's the cause of all the hubbub. He begins to sweat a little."

"All right, he's sweating a little."

"The Superior Officer Present Afloat—SOPA—sends over a legal officer and an intelligence officer. Our murderer begins to sweat a little more. Then the skipper appoints an investigation board, and the perspiration really begins to flow now."

"This begins to sound like a soap commercial."

"No. Our boy is frightened now. The noose is tightening. And then we come. The Federal Bureau of Investigation." Norton announced it grandly. "Secret agents. The FBI. The dread of all criminals, the nemesis of all evil. So we come to this ship. Bang, everyone is restricted to the vessel. Bang, the crew knows we're taking fingerprints up in the radar shack. Bang, we begin asking questions, and then our questioning begins to get heaviest on three men: Daniels, Schaefer, and Jones. If our murderer is one of them—and I feel certain he is—he's beginning to get a little nervous now. After all, how long can he go on outwitting the almighty FBI?"

"I don't get your point, Fred."

"My point is this: We have nothing on which to convict anyone. Only our murderer, I hope, doesn't know that. He just sees a lot of activity, secret agents coming and going to the ship, quiet, taciturn, except when they're asking questions. This guy is not a professional, Matt. We ask about Wilmington. All right, he knows we know about the Wilmington shackup, and then he begins wondering. Do we know why the nurse was killed? he wonders. As it happens, we don't know—but he doesn't know that. She wasn't pregnant, according to the autopsy. All right, maybe it was just a lovers' quarrel. But something provoked him into action. He knocked off the nurse, and now we're asking questions about Wilmington. How'd we find out about

Wilmington? One of the dead nurse's girl friends? If so, how much did Claire Cole tell? Is his identity known? How tight is the noose? Are we just playing cat-and-mouse with him? What's the penalty for murder? All these things begin eating at him. In short, Matt, he is goddamned good and scared, and it's just a matter of time before he cracks."

"Cracks! You think he's going to come running to us to confess?"

"He might. Or he might do something that'll point the finger at him."

"Like what?"

"How do I know? Maybe he'll seek out some of the nurses who knew the dead girl. That'll give us something to follow up, at least. Maybe he'll try to jump ship, make a run for it. Who knows? But one way or another, he'll crack. All we've got to do is wait."

"I don't know," Dickason said.

"I *do* know. I've seen amateur killers before. They don't know their asses from their elbows."

"Well, I hope you're right."

"And me, too," Norton said emphatically. "I don't like Norfolk, and I don't like the Navy. The sooner we get back to Washington, the happier I'll be."

"Norfolk's not bad," Dickason said.

"No, but Delia's *good.*"

"Delia? Oh, your wife."

"Yes," Norton said, "my wife."

"So why bother checking these hotels and rooming houses?" Dickason asked, disturbed. "I mean, what's the sense?"

"It may make the job shorter. Someone may just possibly recognize the photos. And if they don't, we just wait. Our killer will make his move soon, you'll see. They always do, one way or another. When the guilt gets too heavy for them, when they begin to think the whole damn world is against them—bang! They crack."

"They crack," Dickason repeated.

"Here's a shop," Norton said. "Let's get that coffee."

5

HE WAS QUITE PLEASED WITH THE WAY HE'D COME through all the questioning. They really had nothing to go on, of course, except the fact that he'd been at the hospital. Well, he'd handled that nicely, he thought. With both the FBI and Mr. Masters.

There were undoubtedly a good many ways to react to questioning. The point, naturally, was not to appear suspicious, and you could do that by being arrogant about the whole thing, or by being innocent about it. He'd made his choice and then stuck to it, keeping up the pose all along.

They did suspect him. There was no question about that. But they suspected two others as well, and you can't hang a man on suspicion. Somehow they'd learned about that Wilmington week end with Claire. Knowing how Claire had felt about the whole thing, knowing now in retrospect, he was fairly certain she had not discussed it with anyone. The Wilmington information must have been a slip, then, something she'd done or said unawares. Yes, they knew Claire had met someone in Wilmington on that week end. He didn't care how they'd found out. That they knew was enough for him.

And once they knew, they'd undoubtedly checked the ship's liberty list, and then checked that against the list of men who'd been to the hospital recently, men who'd had a chance to know Claire. He'd turned up as a possible suspect. But that was the extent of it. He was sure they didn't know more than that. If they did, they'd have already pulled him in.

He had never been seen together with Claire, and that

was definitely in his favor. Oh, yes, they'd been very careful about that angle. It had been necessary at the time. You couldn't expect a j.g. to go running around with an enlisted man. But it was all working to his advantage now, and that was fine.

Even the Wilmington thing had been completely under wraps. Claire had gone earlier by bus and train, and he had followed later. She had taken a room at the David Blake, telling the desk clerk she was expecting her husband later in the day. She'd registered as Mr. and Mrs. Mark Knowles. She'd had luggage. She looked respectable; Claire always *had* looked respectable. There'd been no questions asked.

When he arrived in Wilmington, he called the hotel and asked for Mrs. Mark Knowles. Claire had come to the phone breathless.

"Claire? Honey? I'm here."

"Oh, baby, I'm so glad."

"Why? Was it difficult?"

"No, no. No trouble at all. I'm just lonely."

"Well, I'm here."

"Good. Are you coming up?"

"Yes. What's the room number?"

She'd given him the number. He'd left the pay phone and gone directly to the hotel. He did not stop at the desk. He went straight to the elevator banks and up to Claire's floor. He waited until the elevator door closed, waited until he heard the lift mechanism whir into motion again. Then he'd gone to the room.

They'd spent most of that week end in the room. Whenever they left the hotel for meals or a walk or a movie, they did so quietly. Claire never left the room key at the desk. They had both worn quiet civilian clothing. They had not become overly friendly with any of the hotel personnel or guests. They were, for all practical purposes, just another nice, quiet married couple stopping over in town for the week end. When they checked out, they did so as quietly and unobtrusively as they'd done everything else. Claire had paid for the room when she'd registered. When they checked out, he took their luggage and went to wait outside. Claire left their key at the desk, thanked the manager for a nice stay, and then left. They walked to the railroad station together. They boarded the train at separate cars, not seeing or speaking to each other again once they'd left Wilmington. It had all gone off without a hitch.

He stood near the fantail now, smelling the faint odor of the garbage cans stacked there, and smelling the deeper, brackish odor of the water slapping the metal skin of the ship. He drew in on his cigarette and thought, I'll get away with it.

He was sure of that. Even with all the questioning, even with all the secret horse manure, he knew he would get away with it. He was sure no one in Wilmington would remember either Claire or him. They'd given no one anything to remember. Yes, he would get away with it.

The thought didn't please him, because he liked it better with her alive. She'd been something, all right. She'd certainly been something. Right from the start. One of those things where two people just click suddenly. That spark, sort of, flaring up in two pairs of eyes. She was officer's stuff, all right, but she'd been all his. He thought of her body again, thought of it in his arms, thought of it as he'd seen it on that Wilmington week end. The thought pained him. She had been so much woman, more woman than he'd ever had before. Why'd she have to turn stupid on him? Why couldn't she have let things roll along the way they were going? Christ, it had been a perfect setup, and they'd been good together.

Well, there were other women, that was something you could always count on. Women. No matter what else failed, no matter how hard the Navy hopped on you, there were always women. And once you got off the goddamned ship, even in a sad town like No Curse Nor Drink Norfolk, he'd always managed to make out. You could count on women. Still, Claire had been something better than most women.

Maybe he'd pull another hospital stint, get to meet another nurse. Hey, now, that wasn't such a bad idea. After this was all over, of course. This damn restricted crap was beginning to wear on him. How long can you keep a guy cooped up? This was worse than boot camp. But that hospital idea was a good one. Hell, it had worked before, why not again? Sure, when this was all over. After all the Hawkshaws got through snooping around. Mr. Masters handed him a laugh, all right. Firing questions like a D.A. in court. Where was this, and when was that, and blah-blah-blah. A real laugh.

Those FBI characters were a pretty good comic routine themselves. Abbott and Costello, or Martin and Lewis. Hell, they couldn't find the *Missouri* if someone hid it in their shower stall.

He chuckled at his own humor, took a last drag on the cigarette, and then flipped it over the side, watching it arc against the blackness of the sky, and then hiss momentarily when it struck the water.

The FBI boys had returned to the ship at around 2100. It was 2230 now, and he still hadn't been called for further questioning, so he was willing to bet they hadn't turned up anything new. He was safe. This was one cookie they weren't going to grab. He chuckled again, and was turning to go when he heard the footsteps coming toward him. He panicked for just a moment and then he told himself, Easy. Easy now.

He squinted his eyes against the darkness, wishing someone would open the hatch to the aft sleeping compartment so he'd have some light to see by. The figure was closer now, and he still couldn't identify it. Maybe Masters coming to ask some more questions. Or maybe Martin and Lewis again. Maybe they *had* turned up something. Maybe . . . No, no, they couldn't have. No one knew he'd gone to Wilmington. No one had seen him. He was safe.

"Who's there?" he asked the darkness.

"Me."

"Who's me?"

"Schaefer."

"Oh. What do you want?"

He watched Schaefer move closer, and he clenched his fists, prepared for whatever was coming. Schaefer moved noiselessly, stepping close to the garbage cans. He watched him warily.

"I was just about to turn in," he said.

"That can wait," Schaefer answered.

"Sure," he said. He speared a single cigarette from the pocket on his denim shirt, changed his mind and let it drop back into the package again. "What's on your mind, Schaefer?"

"The dead nurse," Schaefer said softly.

He felt his hands shake a little, and he controlled the tremble and asked, "What about the dead nurse?"

"You know," Schaefer said.

He looked around the fantail quickly. There was no one else on deck back there. The stern of the ship was in complete darkness.

"No," he answered slowly. "I don't know."

"At the hospital," Schaefer said. "You and the nurse."

"I don't know what you're talking about."

"You know, all right. I was in the bed opposite yours, and I saw you playing up to her. I saw you, so don't deny it."

His mind raced back. Had Schaefer really been in the bed opposite? Or was this one of Mr. Masters' tricks?

"All right," he said cautiously, "I played up to her. So what?"

"You went to Wilmington, too," Schaefer said. "On your week end. I know that."

"You're crazy."

"No, I'm not crazy. I know because you asked for a Wilmington train schedule at the office a few days before that week end. I remember that. I was typing up the promotions list when you asked for it. I remember."

"You're crazy," he said again, but he was thinking furiously now, trying to remember. Had he asked for a Wilmington schedule? Why the hell had he done that? Yes, yes, he remembered now. He *had* asked. Claire thought it would be safer for him to get the information aboard ship. A lot less conspicuous then her checking on it ashore, and men gossiped a lot less than women. Yes, he'd asked for the schedule, and Schaefer,— that sonofabitch—remembered.

"So what? What are you driving at, Schaefer?"

"Mr. Masters thinks there's a connection. I shut up before now because I didn't want to be a squealer."

"You mean you told Masters all this crap?"

"No. Not yet. But if you killed that nurse . . ."

He lashed out suddenly with his bunched fist, catching Schaefer on the point of his jaw. Schaefer staggered back a few paces, crashing into one of the garbage cans. He hit Schaefer again, and this time the man went limp, falling to the deck.

He was breathing harshly when he bent down for Schaefer. He looked over his shoulder, thankful when he saw no one there. He picked the man up then, dragged him past the garbage cans and to the fantail. He lifted him over the chains dangling there and then released him. He waited until he heard the body splash into the water.

Then he shouted, "Man overboard! Man overboard!" and he ran down the starboard side of the ship, climbing the ladder to the boat deck and merging with the shadows. Behind him, he could hear the men rushing up out of the aft sleeping compartment.

At 2247 on 4 November, Richard N. Schaefer, Y 2/c, USNR, leaped to his death from fantail of U.S.S. *Sykes.* Cry of "Man overboard" brought men from aft sleeping compartment to scene of suicide. Hooks and grapples were used to recover body which was retrieved from water after one hour, thirteen minutes, difficulty arising because body had lodged itself beneath ship's screw. Artificial respiration was administered, but Schaefer was pronounced dead by *Sykes'* chief pharmacist's mate at 0016, later corroborated by physician from hospital ashore.

Dickason and Norton were in wardroom with Commander Glenburne at time of suicide, discussing negative findings on Wilmington field trip. Afterward, at scene of suicide, Dickason noted bruises on Schaefer's jaw and cheekbone, these later attributed to contact with ship's screw when body struck water and was carried toward ship by current. Paint scrapings on Schaefer's wrist watch affirm contact with ship.

As noted in our report 32-A-741, dated 1 November, Schaefer was one of the prime suspects in death of Lt. (j.g.) Claire Cole. Without benefit of scientific data, we were forced to piece together circumstantial evidence:

a) Schaefer knew Miss Cole, having made her acquaintance while confined to base hospital in late September of this year.

b) Schaefer had access to Combat Information Center (radar shack) key, which is available in Ship's Office.

c) Schaefer was on week end liberty same week end in which Cole kept alleged rendezvous with unidentified sailor.

Our contention is that Schaefer, driven by guilt, haunted by fear of exposure, took his life by simplest means at hand. Records reveal that Schaefer was expert swimmer, but we believe he swam under fantail, lodging himself beneath screw. Shipmates agree he was acting strangely since death of nurse and ensuing investigation. Therefore respectfully request permission to close files on case and permit commanding officer Glenburne to resume normal activity aboard *Sykes.*

FREDERICK NORTON (agent)

Dickason handed the signed report to Norton.

"Did you read it?" Norton asked.

"Yes. Yes, I read it."

"Well?"

"Gee, I don't know, Fred."

"What do you mean, you don't know?"

"Well, I don't know if I'm convinced yet."

"For Christ's sake, Matt—"

"Oh, all right, I know you've had a lot of experience in this sort of thing, but I still don't know, Fred."

"What's the trouble? What's bothering you now, little boy?"

"Nothing. I guess it's the only conclusion we can draw, but I still wish there was something more to go on. No fingerprints, no nothing, and a million damn people crawling all over the ship when the nurse was killed. I just hope we have the right man, Fred."

"You worry too goddamn much," Norton said. "In something like this, you've got to take the facts as they fall. I told you the killer would crack, didn't I?"

"Yes, you did."

"Well, he cracked. Look, Matt, I agree, either Daniels or Jones could have killed the goddamned nurse, too. But it was Schaefer that jumped off the fantail! You tack that onto the rest we've got, and he's our man."

"Yeah, I suppose."

"Do you like this Navy horse manure?" Norton said.

"No. Of course not."

"Do you want to go back to Washington?"

"Yes."

"Then you want some advice? Forget it. This is only one case, and not a very important one, at that."

"Well, I don't want to seem like an eager beaver . . ."

"Then don't."

"Is this standard operating procedure?"

"Nothing is standard operating procedure. You fit the facts to the case. As far as I'm concerned, Schaefer conclusively proved his guilt by taking his own life. That's good enough for me."

"But if reasonable doubt exists, shouldn't we investigate further?"

"What reasonable doubt?"

"Well . . ." Dickason hesitated.

"See? There really isn't any doubt in your mind. Admit it. Would you kill yourself if you hadn't done anything?"

"I guess not."

"All right, then. Sign the damned report, and let's get it off. With a little luck, we'll be back in Washington before the week is out."

MR. FREDERICK NORTON
HOTEL FIELDS
NORFOLK, VIRGINIA
RETURN WASHINGTON FOR FURTHER ORDERS. ADVISE
COMMANDER GLENBURNE RESUME NORMAL ACTIVITY
ABOARD SYKES. CONSIDER FILE CLOSED.
                              SALVATORE D'OGLIO
                              FIELD DIRECTOR

MR. AND MRS. PETER SCHAEFER
831 EAST 217 STREET
BRONX 67, NEW YORK
THE MEN AND OFFICERS OF THE USS SYKES, DD 012,
WISH TO EXPRESS THEIR SINCERE SYMPATHY ON THE
DEATH OF YOUR SON RICHARD SCHAEFER. AS THE WAR
DEPARTMENT INFORMED YOU AN ACCIDENT OF THIS NA-
TURE IS EXTREMELY RARE AND ITS OCCURRENCE IS THUS
DOUBLY SHOCKING. YOUR SON'S PERSONAL EFFECTS
WILL BE FORWARDED WITHIN A MATTER OF DAYS AND
MEANWHILE BE CERTAIN WE SHARE YOUR LOSS DEEPLY.
                              JONAS R. GLENBURNE
                              CMDR., USNR

"It's disgusting," Masters said. "The old bastard sounds actually gleeful."

"He had to send a wire," Reynolds said. He shrugged. "He was good enough to leave out the fact that Schaefer was a goddamn murderer."

"*If* he was a murderer," Masters said.

"The FBI seems to think so. Look, Chuck, let it lie. The nurse's home town is happy and CinCLant is happy, and the Squadron Commander is happy, and most of all the Old Man is happy. Let it lie."

"Sure, let it lie."

"What's the matter?"

"Nothing."

"No, what's the matter? You think Schaefer didn't do it?"

"Didn't do what? Didn't commit suicide, or didn't kill the nurse?"

"Take your choice."

"I don't think he did either."

"How so?"

"Did you see his effects? I did."

"I saw them."

"All right. If you saw them, you know Schaefer was in the middle of a letter to his folks. The letter was dated the night of the alleged suicide. Now, you can't tell me that a guy who's ready to leap over the fantail is going to stop a letter in the middle of a sentence and then take his swim—without even mentioning anything to his own parents."

"Not all suicides leave notes."

"No. But most suicides like to leave things in some state of order. Hell, Schaefer had his soap and towel laid out on his sack."

"What's your theory?"

"Who the hell knows? Maybe he was troubled by something. Maybe he left the letter to take a walk, or maybe he went to the head. Maybe he saw someone and stopped to talk to him. Maybe somebody shoved him over the fantail."

"I doubt it. I doubt it very much, Chuck."

"Yeah? Well, maybe you should take a look at his records. And then maybe you can tell me why a guy like Schaefer chose drowning as his means of suicide."

"I don't get it," Reynolds said, puzzled.

"You don't, huh? Well, it's all in his records. Schaefer

was an expert swimmer. As a matter of fact, he applied for underwater demolition school when he first entered the Navy. Now you tell me how an expert swimmer expects to drown by jumping over the side!''

''Well . . .''

''Think it over, Mike. And think over motives while you're at it. Let's assume Schaefer did kill the nurse. If he's caught, the Navy hangs him. That's the penalty for murder, isn't it?''

''Yes.''

''All right, all he had to lose is his life, right? He's in the reserve, so he really doesn't give a damn about a Navy career or honors or glory or what the hell have you. He's just putting in time, waiting to get back into civvies. If he gets away with the murder, he's out of the Navy and free. If he doesn't, he hangs and loses his life. That's all he can lose; his life. A man smart enough to kill Claire Cole would also be smart enough to take the gamble. But Schaefer didn't, or at least you're telling me he didn't. He took his own life, the only thing he had to lose.'' Masters paused. ''I'm sorry. I don't buy it.''

''What do you buy?''

''I buy a murderer still walking around this goddamned tub. Only now the score is two, and everything is all smoothed out. Activity resumed, nobody restricted to the ship any more. That sonofabitch must be in seventh heaven right now. It burns me up. It makes me sore that some-body thinks he can get away with something like this. And it makes me sorer to think of the meatheads up the chain of command who are tickled pink over Schaefer's alleged suicide.''

''Stop calling it 'alleged,' Chuck. CinCLant—''

''CinCLant, my bloody foot! CinCLant is just as tickled as everyone else. Now the pressure's off, and everybody can relax. Everybody can go on bucking for his fourth stripe or a few more scrambled eggs on his hat. Everybody can go to the Officers' Club and drink a toast to the bril-liant investigation board. And everybody can forget all about a dead nurse, and a poor slob who lived in the Bronx! It stinks! For two cents, I'd—"

"Take it easy, Chuck. The case is closed."

"I know."

"There's nothing more to be done."

"I know."

"Just relax, Chuck."

"That's just what I'm going to do. I'm going to the Club tonight, and I'm going to get stinking blind."

6°

IT IS VERY PLEASANT HERE, MASTERS THOUGHT.

I like the lighting, and I like the soft music, and I even like the background of muted voices. Most of all, I like the Scotch. You have to hand it to the Navy, they certainly know how to choose Scotch.

And Scotch is a miraculous cure-all, a medicine for the soul. He grinned and twirled the liquid in his glass, listening to the ice cubes clink against its side. It even tastes like medicine the first few times, he thought. Only the first few times. After that, you get used to it, and the bloody stuff has no taste any more, and that's the highest recommendation you can give any medicine.

He wondered if there were Scotch aboard for medicinal purposes. No, brandy, it would be—and the pharmacist's mates had probably consumed all that a long time ago. Pity the poor bastard who fell overboa . . .

Well, now, he thought, here we are back again. Like a merry-go-round, Lieutenant Masters. Around and around, and always back to that poor sonofabitch yeoman who got shoved off the fantail.

One of them did it, that was certain. Either Jones, the radarman, or Daniels, the other yeoman. That was for certain. Now, if this wasn't the Navy, we would take both those bastards and beat them black and blue until one of them confessed. If this wasn't the Navy. But this *is* the Navy, Lieutenant Masters. God, you should certainly know that.

Yes, I most certainly do know that. This is the Navy, and the case is closed, and we're ready to start another case, Scotch this time. Don't you ever want to become a lieutenant commander, Lieutenant Masters? If you do, drink up and forget Claire Cole, and forget Richard Schaefer, and go about your business. Drink up.

Eat, drink and make Mary, for tomorrow . . . Tomorrow. Oh, well, tomorrow. Where's Mary *now?* That's the important question before the big investigation board. Where's Mary now?

He sipped a little more Scotch, aware of the fact that his head was becoming a little muddled and his thinking a bit unclear. He drained the glass and looked around the dimly lighted room and his mind echoed, Where's Mary? The hell with Mary, he thought. I don't even know any Mary. It's time for another Scotch. Scotty, that's who I know. He got unsteadily to his feet and made his way to the bar. He plunked down his glass and said, "Scotch and water, please. And go easy on the ice cubes."

"Yes, sir," a voice answered.

Yes, sir, yes, sir, three bags full. One snoot full that's all I need. Where the hell's that Scotch?

"Hey!" he called.

"Coming, sir."

"Yeah, well, today, not sometime next year."

"Here you are, sir. Scotch and water, easy on the ice."

Easy on the eyes, indeed! Who's the punster in our midst? Lowest form of animal life is a punster.

He lifted his face and looked at the man behind the bar, the man who held his drink extended.

"Well, now," he said aloud.

"Sir?"

"Well, now, Mr. Jones. Mr. Radarman Third Class Jones. Well, now, what the hell are you doing serving me drinks?"

Jones smiled and put the tall glass down on the bartop. "You ordered a Scotch and water, sir," he said. His eyes were secretly amused, as if the sight of an officer three sheets to the wind pleased him.

"I know what I ordered, Jones. I know damn well what

I ordered. Now tell me what you're doing behind that bar, Jones. You standing radar watch at the Officers' Club?"

"I swung the duty, sir."

"I thought the duty was reserved for steward's mates and such, Jones."

Jones winked slyly. "Not if you know the right people, sir."

"And you know the right people, huh? Who are these right people, Jones?"

"Connections, sir. A ship ain't all spit and polish, you know."

"Maybe I should know your connections, huh, Jones? Maybe I'd stop getting mid-watches, huh?"

Jones smiled again. "Maybe, sir."

"Tell me, Jones. What's so special about Club duty? How come you need connections to get it?"

Jones shrugged. "You know, sir."

"No, I don't know. I honestly do not know, so help me. Tell me, Jones."

"Well, there's liquor around, you know."

"Ahhh, liquor."

"Yes, sir."

"Am I to believe that you have been copping a nip now and then, Jones?"

"Did I say that, sir?" Jones was grinning broadly at him now.

"No, you did not. You very carefully did not say that. You're a smart cookie, Jones."

"Thank you, sir."

"A very smart cookie. You and the other one, only one is smarter than both of you together. He'd have to be to do what he did and do it the way he did it. He's the real smart one. Are you the real smart one, Jones?"

"Sir?"

"You see, that's very smart. Pretend ignorance. Very smart. You're smart, all right, Jones."

A Wave officer staggered to the bar and banged her glass down on the top. She was a redhead, and she'd taken off her jacket, and her blouse hung out of her skirt in the back.

"Hey, Jonesy," she called. "Le's have a little service."

"Yes, ma'am," Jones said. He waked down the bar to the Wave, smiled, and took her glass. "The same, ma'am?"

"I'm a miss, not a ma'am," the Wave complained.

"Yes, miss. The same?"

"The same, Jonesy."

Well, Masters thought, here's Mary now. God, is that Mary?

Jones poured a whisky sour and brought it to the Wave, setting it down before her. The Wave took the drink, threw off half of it, and then leaned forward, her breasts pressing against the edge of the bar.

"You're cute, you know, Jonesy?"

"Thank you, ma'am."

"Miss, not ma'am. I'm a miss, Jonesy. Remember that."

"I will, miss."

"Good. You goddamn better well remember it, 'cause I outrank you in spades."

"Yes, miss," Jones nodded.

"In spades." She nodded her head in accord with herself swept the glass from the bar, and walked with drunken dignity back to her table in the corner.

Masters said, "Nice, huh, Jones?"

"Sir?"

"The broad."

"Oh. Yes, sir, if you say so, sir."

"Is that another reason Club duty is desirable, Jones?"

"The broads, you mean?" Jones shrugged. "Officers' stuff, sir, not for the lowly."

"You sound bitter, Jones."

"Me? Perish it, sir. I'm the world's happiest."

"Why?"

"I just am. Why be bitter. Things are tough all—"

"Yeah, I know."

"You want another drink, sir?"

"No. Thanks, Jones. I think I'll see if I can't find Mary."

"Who, sir?"

"You wouldn't know her, Jones. Officers' stuff."

He turned and put his elbows on the bar, and then began a methodical scrutiny of the room. The Wave with the whisky sour was sitting with a commander, so that was out; she sure as hell was not Mary, not for Masters, anyway. He kept turning his head in short jerks, scrutinizing the place the way he'd scan the horizon for an enemy ship. Perfect lookout procedure, he thought.

When he saw her, he didn't recognize her at first. She was in dress uniform, and he remembered her in starched white. But he was glad to see her, and he was surprised she was sitting alone.

He lifted his glass and walked across the room, trying to maintain his sense of balance. She was toying with her drink, and she did not see him as he approached. When he reached her table, he cleared his throat.

"Miss Dvorak," he said. "Jean Dvorak."

She seemed flustered, and he hoped to hell she wouldn't blush. Only roses should blush, not women. "Hello, Mr. Masters," she said.

"Chuck," he reminded her. "May I sit down?"

"Well . . ."

She hesitated and looked around the room, and he quickly asked, "Or are you with someone?"

She bit her lower lip. "Well, I was. But she seems to have disappeared or something."

Masters sat down. "She?" he asked.

"Yes. She."

He grinned, and Jean Dvorak grinned back, and her face opened again, and he knew he'd never get over what a smile could do for her.

"You should smile more often," he said.

"Really? Why?"

He nodded his head. "That was the proper answer.

When a gentleman gives a cue for a compliment, the lady should always supply the proper answer. That was the proper answer.''

Jean blushed, and he felt instantly sorry for what he'd said. "I'm sorry," she said softly. "I had no intention of being coy."

"Nor I of being a cavalier. You should smile more often because you're quite beautiful when you do."

"Thank you," she said.

"Not at all. What are you drinking?"

She looked down at her drink as if seeing it for the first time. "Oh, I really don't know," she said, seemingly flustered again. "Mary ordered it for me. She's the one who was—"

"Mary!" He opened his eyes wide, and then the laugh bubbled from his mouth. "Mary! Oh, God, no. Oh, God, that can't be true. Mary! Well, no wonder she's lost."

Jean looked bewildered. "I'm sorry, I don't understand."

"A private gag," Masters said. "Forgive me, it was rude."

"That's quite all right."

"No, really. I'm very sorry. It was a personal joke, and a somewhat low one, at that."

"That's all right."

"And I'm forgiven?"

"Really, there's no need for—"

"Say I'm forgiven. Please do."

She smiled, and he unconsciously smiled back. "You're forgiven."

"Good. Excellent. I feel much better."

"I'd say you were feeling pretty good to begin with."

"Scotch," he said. "The cure-all. I'm drowning my sorrows."

"Your sorrows?"

"The postsuicide blues."

"Oh. That boy on your ship."

"Yes."

"I saw it in the base newspaper. It was terrible, wasn't it?"

"More so than you think."

"I don't understand."

"The wrong man, sweetheart. The wrong man."

She wrinkled her forehead, and he said, "Please don't do that."

"What?" she asked.

"Your forehead, the wrinkles. They'll stay that way."

"Oh. I'm sorry. What did you mean about the wrong man?"

"Forget it. It's all part of the postsuicide blues." He looked at her and said, "You're doing it again. You'll be sorry when you're forty."

"You mean you think he's not the one who murdered Claire?"

"Ah. Yes, that's what I think. Or that's what I think I think. Listen, do we have to stay here? Don't all these commanders and captains and assorted brass give you the willies?"

"Well . . ."

"I know. Don't say it. You're waiting for Mr. Right. I saw it on your face that day I asked you for dinner. O.K., apologies extended. I'll fold my Scotch like the Arabs and silently steal away."

She giggled suddenly, and then covered her mouth. "You're really quite amusing when you're . . . when you're this way, you know. Forgive me, I shouldn't have laughed."

"Honey," he said, "your laugh outdistances your smile." He frowned. "That's a hard word to say, the way I feel. Outdistances. Which is what I shall do right now. Thanks for the use of your table, Miss Dvorak."

He stood, and she put her hand on his sleeve.

"No, don't go," she said. "It's all right."

He stared down at her. "What's all right?"

"I mean . . ."

"You mean you'll come with me? We'll leave all these

stripe-happy bastards, pardon me, behind and seek some fresh air that doesn't stink of the Navy?''

She giggled again. "Well, I wasn't going to put it exactly that way.''

"Ma'am,'' he said, "miss, Jean, there's only one way to put it. Only one way. Let's get the hell out of here, but first let me say good-by to a remaining third of the triumvirate.''

"My heaves, who's that?''

"He poses now as Bacchus, but he may really be Morpheus.''

"Morpheus?''

"The guy who puts people to sleep. I'll be right back.''

He staggered across the room and stopped in front of the bar.

"Hey, Jones,'' he said. "Hey, Jones, you bastard, c'mere.''

Jones moved over to Masters warily. "Yes, sir?''

"Don't 'yes' me, and don't 'sir' me. Just remember this, you bastard. I'll be watching you. I got nothing to do on that goddamned ship, anyway, so I'll be watching you. With all my eyes, Jones. Every one of them. I'll be watching you and that other sonofabitch, and God help either of you the first time you step out of line. Just remember that.''

Jones eyes Masters levelly. "Why've you got the knife in me, sir?'' he asked.

"Hah!'' Masters snorted. He turned and reeled across the room, taking Jean's arm and leading her to the door.

"I warned him,'' he said. "I warned the bastard. Now I'll watch him. Him and Daniels. Come on, Jean, miss, ma'am. I got a jeep out here someplace.''

"Do you think you should drive? I mean . . .''

"No, I shouldn't,'' Masters said. "But I will anyway. Do you fear for your life?''

"No,'' she said in a small voice.

"You do. You do, and it's sweet of you to say you don't.

Come on, we'll walk." He paused. "I haven't got a jeep, anyway. Where the hell would I get a jeep?"

They walked down the tree-lined streets of the base. The barracks were unlighted, and the trees cast large shadows on the brick walls.

"This is a beautiful base," he said. "One of the prettiest."

"Yes, it is."

"It's a shame it's in such a rat town. Rat towns shouldn't have beautiful bases."

"They shouldn't."

"My bit of philosophy for the day," he said. "Where are we walking?"

"I don't know. I'm following you."

"Well, there are a variety of things available on this lovely base. We can wander around and look at the trees and the flowers. Would you like to do that?"

"If you want to."

"Or we can stroll over to the air base and watch the Navy pilots make landings in the dark. That is apt to be dangerous."

"Then let's not do it."

"You do not, I gather, appreciate danger."

"Sometimes."

"Fine. There then remains a magnificent ball field, complete with bleachers and tons of grass. The weather is uncommonly mild, and we can pretend there is a game in progress. What say?"

She hesitated. "I don't know."

"It is restricted," he went on. "But methinks a mere enlisted man guards the portals. We can scare him away with all our associated bars, Ensign Dvorak."

"All right," she said, and then she laughed softly and held his arm tighter. They walked in silence until the outline of the ball field loomed ahead. Standing near the gate was an enlisted man with a guard belt and a rifle.

Masters walked over and said, "You there! Snap to!"

The man leaped to attention. "Sorry, sir. I—I didn't see you."

"That's a fine recommendation for a man on watch. I saw some Waves in their underwear trying to crawl under the fence at the far end of the field. Get over there and stop them."

"Yes, sir." The guard started running, and Jean began laughing.

"He must think you're crazy," she said.

"No. But he's going to be mighty disappointed. After you, m'dear."

They walked across the field, and he took off his jacket, over her protests, and spread it on the ground for her. They sat, and the stars were etched sharply overhead, and the world seemed to end at the perimeter of the ball field.

"I'm beginning to get sober," he said.

"Are you? Well, good."

"Why? I'm also beginning to remember why I got looped."

"Schaefer again?"

"Schaefer again. Damnit, why'd they have to stick me on that damned investigation board?"

"Chuck, can't you forget it? You know the Navy as well as I do. Look at it this way. How many men are killed when a ship goes down?"

"Sure."

"Chuck . . ."

"Yes?"

"You're not going to get morose, are you?"

"No, I'm not." He laughed suddenly.

"What's that for?"

"Mary. I was just thinking of Mary."

"My girl friend?"

"No. Another Mary. A girl whom you are not—but I think I'll kiss you anyway."

"Chuck . . ."

He took her in his arms, and she tried to hold him away for just a moment, until his mouth found her. And then she trembled slightly in the circle of his embrace and gave her lips to him.

"I'll be seeing a lot of you, you know," he said.

"I . . ."

"Yes, I will. Oh, yes, I will. You might as well get used to the way I kiss."

She caught her breath, and when she spoke, her voice was very low. "I'm used to it already," she said.

7

MASTERS HEARD REVEILLE SOUNDED OVER THE SHIP'S P.A.
system the next morning, but it didn't get him out of his
sack. He heard Le Page come grumbling awake in the
bunk opposite him. He rolled over, his face to the bulkhead, pulling the pillow over his head. Le Page shuffled
around for his shoes, and Masters wondered why the hell
they'd put a meathead like the Ensign in with him. A man
should be quiet in the morning. A man should come to
terms with life again slowly. He shouldn't tumble around
until life slapped him right in the face like a wet mackerel.

What the hell was Le Page doing now? Masters could
hear the rattle of his dog tags, and beneath that another
sound he couldn't immediately identify. He placed it then,
and he was tempted to throw his pillow at Le Page's empty
head. The goddamn jackass was making up his sack!

"Hey, Masters," Le Page said. "Wake up, Masters.
Reveille."

Masters played dead. Maybe if he lay still, without
moving a muscle, without breathing, Le Page would go
away. Maybe Le Page would wander out to the boat deck
and jump over the side.

"Hey, Masters!" Le Page shouted. "Come on, boy.
Reveille! Don't want to miss chow."

From under the pillow and the blanket, Masters omi-
nously intoned, "Le Page, you are a goddamned jackass."

"You awake, Masters?" Le Page asked, apparently
having heard the sullen mumble from beneath the bed-
clothes.

Masters held his breath.

"You awake?" Le Page repeated.

"Yes, goddamnit, I am awake!" Masters shouted. "A dead man couldn't sleep in here with all the goddamn racket you're making."

"Well, gee, Chuck," Le Page said, "I thought you wanted chow."

"I don't want chow," Masters said.

"Well, how was I to know?"

"I don't want anything. I just want silence. Complete silence," Masters said. "I just want to sleep a little."

"A rough night last night?" Le Page asked.

"I don't want an hour-long discussion," Masters said patiently. "I want to sleep. Go, Le Page. Go eat your chow. Eat my helping, too. Eat until you're gorged. Eat until you bust! But just get the hell out of here and leave me alone!"

"Well, sure, Chuck. I mean, if you want—"

"That's an order!" Masters roared.

"Yes, sir," Le Page said. He scurried for the curtained doorway, and Masters smiled grimly and rolled over again.

He closed his eyes and tried to capture sleep again, but it was no use. He was awake. Well, I'm awake, he thought. Well, another goddamn day blooming on the horizon. Well, what's so special about . . .

Jean. Jean Dvorak.

The name popped into his mind, and he suddenly remembered everything that had happened the night before, and a smile blossomed involuntarily on his face. He nodded in satisfaction. A nice girl. A real nice girl, one of the nicest he'd ever run across. Had he promised to call her today?

He didn't remember. But he would call her, whether he'd promised or not, as soon as he could get off the ship. In that case, he thought, leave us get the hell out of our sack.

He swung his legs over the side of his bunk and scratched his chest idly, listening to the rattle of his dog tags. He yawned cavernously, stretched his muscular arms over his head, and then sighed.

His blues were thrown over the back of a metal chair, looking rumpled and disconsolate. He abruptly remembered all the Scotch he'd drunk the night before. Drunk was the word for it, all right. He wondered if he'd behaved all right with Jean. Yes, he was pretty sure he had. Be a hell of a thing to mess up with a girl like that. You don't run across a girl like that every day of the week.

"Tor-ay-oh-dor," he sang suddenly, "don't spit on the floor. Use the cuspidor. That's what it's for."

Of course, this did not apply to a Naval vessel. There were no floors on a Navy vessel. There were only decks. "Tor-ay-oh-dor," he sang again, "don't spit on the deck. Use Le Page's neck. Make the low-down sonofabitch a wreck."

He smiled and pulled on his gray trousers. He went to the sink and washed his face. How many songs like that were there? he wondered, and then he wondered why he was so concerned with things musical this morning. Songs that could be twisted around, of course.

"My Devotion." There was one.

"My abortion," he sang, "was painful, and cost me a fortune . . ."

That was an old one. He'd learned it years back when the song was popular. He'd learned another one at that time, too, and it was probably the most disgusting distortion he'd ever heard. It was a take-off on "Jealousy."

Leprosy, he sang silently, you're making a mess of me. There goes my right ear. There goes my left ear.

He brushed his teeth vigorously, taking the taste of the song and the preceding night's Scotch out of his mouth. Does Le Page ever wash? he wondered. I think all the sonofabitch does is eat. I don't think he's taken a shower since he came aboard. Someday I'll tell him. Le Page, I'll say, I have put up with this godawful stink for a good many moons now, Le Page, my good man.

What godawful stink, Chuck? he will ask.

The godawful stink emanating from your rotund little form, Le Page, I shall answer. I suggest you take a shower, Le Page. I suggest you wash off all the crawling little vermin that are suffocating the opening of your navel and perhaps other apertures, Le Page. I suggest you do that right this minute, Le Page, and in case you were wondering about the strength of my motivations, that is an order, Le Page, that is a goddamned order! Now hop to it!

Someday.

Not now. Not right now. Right now I'm going to the wardroom, where I'll stuff myself full of the garbage they call morning mess, which is exactly what it is. And then quarters for muster, and then I shall sneak away from this floating cracker box and make a call to the nurses' quarters, and perhaps Jean will agree to see me this evening.

He dried his face and hands, flipped the towel onto his sack, and then walked out into the passageway and then onto the main deck. When he got to the wardroom, he studiously avoided sitting next to Le Page. He sat between Reynolds and Carlucci instead, and then he waited for the steward's mate to take his order. There was a choice of eggs this morning. He chose scrambled, and then asked for an immediate cup of coffee, which he downed almost the instant it was poured.

"How do you feel this morning?" Reynolds asked.

"Just dandy," Masters said. "How do you feel?"

"Lousy. I always feel lousy. What I meant, though, you weren't very chipper yesterday."

"That was yesterday. I feel fine today."

"You've forgotten all about dead people?"

"I didn't say that," Masters said.

"Hey," Carlucci said, "how do you rate pancakes, Mike?" He glared at Reynolds' plate, and then looked back to the sunnysides on his own plate.

"I'm executive officer," Reynolds answered, smiling. "I've grown accustomed to the privileges of rank."

"How about spreading the largess a bit?" Carlucci asked.

"You're better off with the eggs," Reynolds answered.

"Where's the Old Man this morning?" Masters asked.

"I think he's still asleep. When have you ever seen him at morning mess, anyway?"

"Never. I was just hoping he'd fallen over the side or something."

"You're too hard on him," Reynolds said seriously. "He's got a lot of headaches."

"Even now that the FBI has cleared up our nasty little scandal? Hell, I thought the Old Man's worries were over."

"How'd you ever get to be an officer, Chuck?" Reynolds asked.

"I brown-nosed my way through boot camp," Masters replied.

"Shake, pal," Carlucci said, starting to eat his eggs, an obvious look of distaste on his face.

"No, seriously," Reynolds said.

"Seriously? Truth is, I wanted to be an FBI man. I—"

"Oh, horse manure."

"God's truth, s'help me. I flunked the course, though. Wretched was that day," Masters said woefully. "But, still being obsessed with the idea of performing a government service, I joined the Navy. The Secretary of the Navy immediately gave me a commission. That's the story, Mike."

"Yeah," Reynolds said dryly.

"And here are my eggs," Masters said. He took the plate from the steward's mate and began eating. He glanced over to where Le Page was seated, marveling at the amount of food the Ensign could stuff into his mouth and apparently swallow without chewing.

Reynolds and Carlucci left before he finished his eggs. He ordered another cup of coffee, sat drinking that and smoking until the boatswain announced quarters for muster. He swallowed the remainder of his coffee, squashed the cigarette in an ash tray, and left the wardroom.

The men he passed seemed happier today. A ship was a funny thing, all right. Nothing but a small community.

A tight little community of men living in extremely close quarters. You find a dead nurse in the radar shack, and the smell of the corpse will most naturally spread to the rest of the ship. People don't like corpses where they live. And nobody likes the idea of a killer roaming the decks, which are the streets of the community that is the ship. Nobody likes that idea at all. So Schaefer put an end to the crew's discomfiture. Schaefer, allegedly, leaped over the fantail. He took the stink of the corpse with him, and he also rid the streets of the killer.

The crew, one-track-minded as it was, probably liked Schaefer better now than they had when he was alive. Schaefer had lifted the pall for them. And he had also, incidentally, lifted the restriction. The crew could go awhoring now. The crew could inhabit the dimly lighted dime-a-dance joints in the city that was Norfolk. Or the crew could shoot their pay at the many penny arcades and shooting galleries. Or the crew could get tattooed, or buy tailor-mades, or spend their time and their money in various other ways, none of which were particularly entertaining.

But would the crew ever stop to wonder whether Schaefer had actually strangled the nurse? Does an ordinary citizen ever wonder about the methods of the police? If a rapist is plaguing a neighborhood, and the police claim they've captured him, does the community still lie awake nights wondering? No. The community relaxes.

The crew had relaxed, too. There were smiles now. There was whistling. The cursing had always been there, but it seemed more forceful now. Things were back to normal.

Almost.

They were not back to normal if either Jones or Daniels was a killer. They were not back to normal at all, if that were the case.

And no one cares but me, Masters thought.

Charles Stanton Masters, protector of the innocent, upholder of the righteous, seeker of justice.

Charles Stanton Masters, Jerk First Class.

I should have stood in bed.

Colombo, the quartermaster first, handed Masters the muster sheet. Colombo was tall and lean, and he always showed up for muster with clear eyes and a smiling mouth. Masters envied that fresh look. He never seemed able to attain it in the morning. The communications crew—consisting of radiomen, radarmen, sonarmen, signalmen, and quartermasters thrown in for good measure—lined up every morning in the space between the aft sleeping compartment hatch and the rail. They faced the sea, and they inevitably faced it bleary-eyed. Masters and Colombo faced the men. On the mornings when Masters was too groggy to read the sheet, Colombo took over. Colombo was never groggy. Aft of this muster spot, the gunnery men lined up between the aft mounts. Elsewhere along the ship, the other members of the crew faced other officers with similar muster sheets.

The names were read off. If a man were AOL or even AWOL, it was T.S. for him. If a man were below catching forty winks, someone would always answer to his name—but only if they knew he was there. The officer always knew that someone else was answering for an absentee. In fact, he usually sent someone down below to rustle him out of his sack.

In addition to checking attendance, the officer usually gave his men pertinent bits of information concerning the ship's day. For example, he told them there would be an inspection at noon. Or he wanted every man in his division to get a haircut that day. Or pay would be distributed at 1500. Or everyone would be restricted to the ship because a dead nurse had been found in the radar shack. Things like that. For this sailor's life was not a simple matter of waking up in the morning and going about your business. There were men who explained exactly how you should go about your business, and Masters was one of these men.

This morning, there was nothing special to say. He read

off the names in his division listlessly, and each man answered with his own peculiar variation of "Here." The variations ranged from "Yah" to "Yo" to "Yay" to "Present" to "On deck" to—in rare moments—"Here." Jones answered to his name by saying "Yo." "Yo" was the saltiest answer. It didn't take a sailor long to catch on to the fact that "Here" was an answer reserved strictly for guys straight out of boot camp. The muster-reading was accomplished without a hitch. Everyone was present and accounted for. The men hung around, slouching wearily, talking among themselves, until the boatswain tooted his pipe and announced cleaning stations. The men dispersed. Colombo took his time. He was a first-class petty officer. First-class petty officers didn't have to rush.

Masters was only a lieutenant, so Masters went back to his sleeping quarters to see just what the hell was on tap for today. Today was the last day for submitting promotions. The list had already been typed up, but additions could be made today before the list was posted. He had already granted his quota of petty officers, but he thought it would be a good idea to give some of the strikers seaman first. He tossed some names around in his head, and then put them on paper. He thought he'd bring them to the Ship's Office, leave them with the yeomen, and then get the hell ashore to make his call to Jean.

He took the starboard side of the ship down to the midships passageway, and then cut in to where the Ship's Office was set in the bulkhead. He leaned on the counter railing and peeked in.

Perry Daniels was sitting at a desk, typing.

"Hello, Daniels," Masters said.

Daniels did not look up until he reached the end of the line and threw the carriage. When he saw Masters, he said, "Oh, hello, Mr. Masters. What can I do for you?"

He shoved back his chair and walked to the counter.

"Few names I want added to the promotions list. From seaman second to seaman first."

"We can take care of that, sir," Daniels said.

"I imagine you've been pretty busy in here, eh, Daniels?"

Daniels looked at Masters levelly. "How do you mean, sir?"

"Now that Schaefer's dead."

"Oh."

"Leaves you a little short-handed, doesn't it?"

"Well, sir, O'Brien has been helping out a lot. He's a striker, but he's probably making third class today. He's a good man."

"Then you don't miss Schaefer at all, eh, Daniels?"

"Oh, no, sir. I didn't say that, sir."

"Did you two get along well? You and Schaefer?"

"Oh, yes, sir," Daniels said. "We never had any trouble. Of course, I never even guessed he was the one killed that nurse. He seemed like such a nice fellow, if you know what I mean."

"Yes, I know what you mean," Masters answered.

"You never can tell, I suppose."

"No, you never can."

"I'll take care of that promotions list for you, sir. Don't worry about it."

"I won't, Daniels. And don't worry about Wilmington."

Daniels' brows lifted just a fraction of an inch. He blinked his eyes and then said, "Sir?"

"We think the fellow who said he saw you there was lying," Masters went on, improvising.

"Somebody said he saw me in Wilmington, sir?" Daniels asked. His complexion had turned a ghastly white, and he kept staring at Masters.

"Yes," Masters said.

"Who? I mean, who would want to say something like that?"

"Why? What difference does it make, Daniels? Nothing wrong with going to Wilmington, is there?"

"Well, no. Hell, no. But I mean, why would I want to go all the way up there?"

"All the way up *where*, Daniels?"

"All the way up to Wilmington."

"I thought you didn't know where it was, Daniels."

"Well, I don't," Daniels said, wetting his lips. "What I meant was, it must be up North someplace, isn't it?"

"Yes," Masters said thoughtfully. "Yes, it is."

"I've got no reason for going up there, sir," Daniels said.

"Not any more, no."

"Sir?"

"Skip it, Daniels. Listen, may I come in and look at some of your records?"

Daniels hesitated again. "Well, uh, sure, if you want to. I . . . I had to see about something anyway. You'll save me the trouble of locking up."

Masters lifted the counter top and stepped into the office. Daniels walked past him and was stepping through the hatch when Masters caught his arm.

"You do know where Wilmington is, don't you, Daniels?" he said.

"No, sir," Daniels answered. "I do not."

"Schaefer's already taken the rap, Daniels. There's no reason to lie any more."

"I don't know what you're talking about, sir," Daniels said.

"Don't you?"

"No, sir. If you'll excuse me, I've got to see someone."

"Sure."

"I'll be back soon, sir. You'll find any keys you need on the board there."

"The key to the radar shack, too?"

"Why, yes. Yes, that key, too."

"All right, Daniels, shove off."

"I'd appreciate it if you hung around until I got back, sir. This won't take a minute."

"Where are you going, Daniels?"

"Well, sir, I loaned a guy my fountain pen, and he

didn't return it. I want to grab him before he forgets and
thinks it's his own."

"I see. You'll handle that promotion stuff for me later?"

"Oh, yes, sir."

"How'd you make out, Daniels?"

"You mean on the promotions list?"

"Yes."

"I haven't seen the yeoman list, sir. Arnecht—he's our
yeoman first—he doesn't like us to see it until it's posted.
I've seen the list for every division, but he's kept the yeomen promotions away from us."

"I see."

"May I go now, sir?"

"Sure, go ahead."

Masters watched Daniels as he crossed the midships
passageway and headed aft. He stood in the hatchway and
wondered why Daniels had lied about Wilmington. He had
sure as hell lied, there was no question about that. Was
Daniels his man? Was Daniels the bastard who'd shacked
up with Claire Cole somewhere in Wilmington? Was he
the one who'd strangled her in the radar shack? Had he
shoved Schaefer overboard? He didn't *look* like a killer.
But neither did Jones, for that matter. And when you got
right down to it, what the hell did a murderer look like?
Shifty eyes? Slack mouth? Sinister nose? Horse manure.

Masters grunted and unlocked the file containing the
service records of every man on the ship. He checked over
Schaefer's record again, looking through the folder, con-
firming what he'd seen earlier. Yes, Schaefer *had* applied
for underwater demolition school. That fact hadn't changed
one damn bit, nossir. He continued looking through the
folder. The yeoman had been twenty-two years old. This
was his first hitch in the Navy, a move probably calculated
to keep him out of the Infantry. Well, that was normal
enough. He kept turning pages. At the end of Schaefer's
folder, the FBI and investigation-board reports terminated
the yeoman's naval career.

Masters sighed and looked through the folders for the

one belonging to Jones, the radarman. Boot camp at Great Lakes. To Fort Lauderdale for radar school. Receiving station in Miami. Destroyer training at Norfolk. Up to Boston for a month's stay at the Fargo Building receiving station. Then to the yards for commissioning of and assignment to the *Sykes*. He'd been with the ship since, up to the time they'd pulled into Norfolk again after their shakedown cruise to Guantanamo Bay, Cuba. Nothing unusual. Never been AOL or AWOL. Never had a captain's mast. An ideal sailor.

Masters grunted and slammed the folder shut. He looked through the pile and pulled out the one belonging to Perry Daniels.

He waded through the introductory garbage, and was ready to turn the page when his eye caught a single item.

"Married."

His eyes sought the typed words again.

"Married."

Christ, that's what it said. Married, married! Perry Daniels was married!

Now hold on a minute, just hold on a minute.

Hadn't he asked Daniels that? Hadn't he asked him the first time he talked to him? Hadn't he said, "Are you married, Daniels?"

And hadn't Daniels answered, "No"?

Well, sure he had. But the records said he was married. The records told Masters that an allotment went to Daniels' wife every month. Now, what the hell . . .

Did Daniels' wife live in Wilmington? Was that why he'd lied about knowing the town, or about being married at all? Had he known about the rendezvous with the dead nurse in Wilmington? Had he known that and lied to keep himself out of hot water?

But how could he have known unless he were a part of that rendezvous?

Now hold it, Masters, let's just hold it a minute. Let's just see where the hell that allotment check goes each month. How about doing that instead of running off half-

cocked? He checked carefully. The allotment went to an
address in North Dakota. It went to Mrs. Perry Daniels.
All right, his wife doesn't live in Wilmington.
All right, let's take it from there.
Let's take an affair with Claire Cole, let's take that if it
agrees with you, Masters. It agrees with me, so let's take
it. Does anyone know about the affair? Well, no, no one
knows about it. Then why the hell lie about Wilmington?
And why lie about being married?
Hell, did anyone aboard ship know that Daniels was
married? Whoever sent the allotment check each month,
naturally. Dave Berson, lieutenant j.g. He sends the allotment checks. He knows Daniels is married. But do any of
the enlisted men know? Do any of Daniels' neighbors—
so to speak—know about it?
Hell, what had Daniels said? He preferred to lone-wolf
it when he was ashore. Well, that figured. If a married
man were going to play around, he didn't want every guy
on the ship to know about it.
That still left the Wilmington lie unexplained. Unless
you drew the obvious conclusion, and that conclusion was
a rendezvous with Claire Cole, an incriminating rendezvous that would point the finger right at Daniels.
Had Claire Cole mentioned anything about a married
man? Had she mentioned it to Jean? If only she'd said
something about it, just dropped something, something
that could be interpreted.
Well, if he'd needed any excuse for calling Jean, this
was it. Damnit, but Daniels was the sly bastard, wasn't
he? Well, sure, it figured. And it provided a possible motive, too. Maybe she threatened to tell the wife all about
it. Now, wait a minute, don't jump to conclusions. Maybe
she didn't threaten a damned thing. Maybe he didn't like
the way she was wearing her lipstick that day. Or maybe
she said something that offended him. Remember that she
was an officer and he was an enlisted man, and that could
have had something to do with it. If Daniels were the man.
And if Daniels weren't the man, why had he lied?

It was worth checking on. It was worth checking on damned fast. He put the folder back into the file, and then left the Ship's Office. Let Daniels worry about the property. That was his headache.

Masters cut through the midships passageway and was heading for the gangway when the squawk box erupted.

"Now hear this. Now hear this. Will all officers report to the wardroom immediately, please? Will all officers report to the wardroom immediately, please?"

Masters snapped his fingers and walked over to Donnelly, who was standing the OD watch.

"What's this all about, Jack?" he asked.

"Search me. The Old Man called it down a few minutes ago. Said to announce it right away."

"Damnit," Masters said.

"You better get up there. His voice held what I laughingly call an urgent undertone."

"His voice always holds an urgent undertone. *God*damnit."

He looked longingly at the gangway. Well, he could call Jean later. He shook his head and walked rapidly to the wardroom, entering without knocking.

Some of the officers were already there, and Masters sidled over to Reynolds and asked, "What's up, Mike?"

"Search me. Probably a cleanliness drive or some damn thing."

"Be just like him," Masters said.

"Listen," Reynolds told him, "you've never had a command. You don't know what it's like."

"You've been in charge of the Atlantic Fleet for years," Masters said, smiling.

"Oh, go to hell," Reynolds answered.

They waited around until everyone had shown up, and then the door opened to admit Commander Glenburne. His eyes were very serious. He wore gray trousers and shirt, with the shirt open at the throat, the silver maple leaves gleaming on his collar.

"At ease, gentlemen," he said. "Please be seated."

They took their places at the table, with the Captain at the head of it. He remained standing, and he placed one hand on the table, the knuckles flat.

"All right, gentlemen," he said, "I'll make this short. We're being turned into a picket ship."

Masters looked up suddenly.

"That's what I said, gentlemen, a picket ship. Some of you may not be familiar with the term, so I'll explain it further. A picket ship scouts ahead of the task force, anywhere from ten to seventy-five miles-out. It forms an airtight screen through the use of radar. We're also using picket ships up in the arctic, to supplement our land-based radar screen there. That's it."

The men remained silent. Glenburne cleared his throat and leaned over the table.

"What does it mean to us? It means our torpedo tubes will be ripped out and replaced by a tripod mast and antenna for altitude-finding radar. It means we'll get jamming gear aboard, probably in the compartment alongside Ship's Service. It means our radarman, radio-technician, and communications-officer complements will practically double in the next few weeks." He looked at Masters. "It means you'll be damned busy from now on, Chuck."

"Yes, sir," Masters said, nodding.

"All right," the Old Man said. "We move into dry dock at eleven hundred today. Work will begin on the ship then. I think this'll be a good time to grant leave to the men, so let's start the ball rolling. Division heads will turn in their leave schedules by fifteen hundred this afternoon. No radarmen on that list of yours, Masters."

Masters frowned. "Why not, sir? I mean . . ."

"I'll explain it to you when the others are gone. I don't want to take up their time now." He glanced at his watch. "We'll get under way at ten hundred. You'll set the watches, Mike."

"Yes, sir."

"Any questions?" He waited. "All right, then. You'd

better get started. If you'll stay, Chuck, we'll go into this further.''

"Yes, sir," Masters said. He remained seated until the other officers cleared the wardroom. Glenburne took out a package of cigarettes and offered one to Masters. Masters took it and lighted it.

"All right, Chuck, this is it. Our new radarmen, Sugar Peter boys mostly, and some men who've had jamming schooling, are already on their way to Brigantine, New Jersey.''

"Where, sir?''

"Brigantine. It's a small island off Atlantic City. The Navy operates a specialized radar training school there. This change means special tactics, Chuck, for both officers and men.''

"I see, sir.''

"The new men are with the new communications officers. You're to meet them there, at the school.''

"When, sir?'' Masters asked.

"You're shoving off as soon as the office can make out your papers. That shouldn't take more than a half hour. That's why I want no radarmen on your leave schedule. They're all going with you.''

"The men won't like it,'' Masters said.

"Tough,'' the Old Man said curtly. "You'd better get started with your packing, Chuck.''

"I'd wanted to go ashore for a minute, sir. I thought—''

"That'll have to wait, I'm afraid.''

"Yes, sir,'' Masters said. "Will that be all?''

"One other thing, Chuck.''

"What's that, sir?''

"About the dead nurse,'' Glenburne said.

"Yes, sir.''

"You're a good officer, Chuck, one of my best. When it comes time for a fitness report, you can be certain you'll get a good one from me.''

"Thank you, sir,'' Masters said.

"I've heard talk I don't like, Chuck. About the nurse. And about you."

"I don't understand, sir."

"Maybe it's just scuttlebutt. If it is, all right, we'll just forget it. If it isn't—well, I thought I should tell you I don't like it. The situation has been cleared up, Chuck. Everybody is finally off my ass, and I want it to stay that way."

"Even if the wrong man—"

"That's just what I mean," Glenburne said, stabbing the air with his forefinger. "Just that kind of talk. Now give a listen here, Chuck. Schaefer killed that nurse. Now you just remember that. Schaefer killed her, and then he committed suicide when the going got too rough. Those are the facts as recorded, and those are the facts as I want them to be."

"You mean you have your doubts, too?"

"No, I haven't any doubts. The Federal Bureau of Investigation is good enough for me. If they say Schaefer did it, he did it. I'm satisfied. Do you get what I'm driving at?"

"I think so."

"All right. I don't want the ashes sifted again. I don't want this damned business repeated. The Squadron Commander has finally cooled down, invited me to a party next week, in fact. If he starts hearing talk about the case being open when it should be closed . . . well, I just don't want him to hear that kind of talk."

"Even if it's true, sir?" Masters asked.

"Goddamnit, Masters, it is not true! Schaefer killed that nurse!"

"I wish I could believe that, sir."

"You'd goddamn well better start believing it, Masters, and damned soon." Glenburne paused, gaining control of himself. "Maybe this Atlantic City trip will clear your head."

"Maybe, sir."

"You're going to be damned busy, Chuck, I told you

that. You're not going to have time to run around playing detective."

"No, sir."

"So put all of this nonsense out of your mind."

"Yes, sir, I'll try, sir."

"Never mind trying, just see that you do, that's all."

"Yes, sir."

"Understand, Chuck . . ." Glenburne paused.

"Sir?"

"Understand that in my mind absolute justice has been done."

"I understand, sir."

Glenburne studied his fingertips. "This . . . ah, ashore. You said you wanted to go ashore for a minute. Is it important?"

"Fairly so, sir."

"A girl?"

Masters hesitated. "Yes, sir."

"I see." Glenburne cleared his throat. "Perhaps . . . perhaps a little diversion is what you need. I mean, to take your mind off this . . . other business."

"Perhaps, sir."

"Had you planned on seeing this girl?"

"Yes, sir, I had hoped to. Before your announcement, of course."

"Of course, your full complement probably won't arrive at Brigantine until tomorrow sometime."

"Oh, is that right, sir?"

"Yes. I thought it might be advisable for you to get there first—you know, sort of get acquainted with the setup." Glenburne considered for a moment. "But if this girl will take your mind off the dead nurse . . ." He paused. "Do you think she might, Chuck?"

Masters smiled at the blackmail attempt. "She might, sir."

"Then why don't we postpone the trip until first thing in the morning? Give the office a little time to get the necessary papers for you and your men, anyway. No sense rushing them, they've been pretty jammed, what with the promotions business, and now the leave schedule. How about that, Chuck? Give you a chance to see this girl of yours.''

"I'd like that, sir," Masters said. "Thank you."

"Not at all," Glenburne said. "You just need a little relaxation, that's all." He smiled fraternally. "Little relaxation never hurt anyone, eh, Chuck?"

"No, sir."

"That's why I always see to it that my men get sufficient leave. A good policy, don't you agree?"

"Oh, yes sir."

The two men were silent for a moment. "Well, there's nothing else on my mind, Chuck," Glenburne said at last.

Masters rose. "Thank you again, sir," he said, starting for the door. When his hand was on the doorknob, Glenburne said, "And Chuck?"

"Yes, sir?"

Glenburne smiled. "Enjoy yourself, boy."

The leave schedule and the promotions list were posted side by side on the bulletin board amidships.

He studied them both very carefully, and then shoved his way through the knot of men crowding the passageway. When he reached the rail, he tossed his cigarette butt over the side.

He walked toward the fantail, and when one of the men greeted him in passing, he did not answer. His mouth was a hard line across his face, and his brows were tightly knotted.

So that's the way it is, he thought. That's the way it's going to be.

He was angry, and the anger showed in his face and in the purposeful strides he took. When he reached the fantail, he sat on one of the depth-charge racks and lighted another cigarette.

Dry dock, he thought. Dry dock while they rip out the goddamn guts of the ship. That's great, just great.

He thought again of the names he'd seen posted on the bulletin board. The thought angered him once more, and he viciously flipped the barely smoked cigarette away.

He was sitting near the fantail, but he did not think of the man he'd thrown overboard so short a time ago. He thought only of his own personal anger, and of officers shoving enlisted men around, and his thoughts made him angrier.

He shoved his hat onto the back of his head, stood abruptly, and headed for the quarter-deck. He'd show them, by Christ! Do that to a man, and you get beans in return. Beans, and cold. He'd show them.

Besides, it was time enough. It was time enough now, and even Masters would be up to his neck with all this conversion. They wouldn't suspect now, and those names on the bulletin board were all he needed to prompt him to action.

He stepped into the passageway amidships and then through the hatch just outside sick bay. The hatch to sick bay was open, and he saw Connerly, one of the pharmacist's mates, inside reading a comic book.

"You open for business?" he asked.

Connerly looked up. He was a young boy with a wild spatter of freckles across his nose and cheeks. He had bright green eyes, and he widened them now and said, "Jesus, you again?"

"I don't feel good," he answered.

"You never do," Connerly said. "You spend more time in the hospital than the medics do."

"If you chancre mechanics did it right the first time," he cracked, "I wouldn't be coming back so often."

"Yeah, yeah. What is it now?" Connerly stood and dumped the comic book onto one of the racks. "You get a dose or something?"

"Don't get smart, Connerly. I think I've got a fever."

"Well, we'll find out," Connerly said wearily. He took a thermometer from where it stood in a jar of alcohol. He wiped the bulb clean with a wad of absorbent cotton.

"You see the lists they posted?"

"What lists?" Connerly asked.

"Amidships. Leave and promotions. Both. Maybe you hit the jackpot, boy."

"No joke? You're not snowing me?"

"No joke," he said. "Go take a look."

"Sure. Here, boy, stick this in your mouth. Three minutes. I'll be back before then. Leaves and promotions, huh? Man!"

Connerly handed him the thermometer and then left the compartment. He waited until Connerly was well out of sight and then he held the thermometer in the palm of his hand and watched the rising silver line of mercury. He took the book of matches from his shirt pocket then, struck one, and held it beneath the bulb of the thermometer. He let the murcury go up to 103 degrees, and then blew out the match. It would probably go down some before Connerly came back. Maybe he should have brought it up to 104. Hell, no. A man's probably dead at 104.

He allowed the bulb to cool slightly, and then put the thermometer back into his mouth. He had it there for thirty seconds when Connerly burst into the compartment.

"Christ, mate!" he said in delight. "I hit second class! And I'm up for leave in two weeks. Brother, how's that?"

He nodded at Connerly, and the pharmacist's mate seemed to remember the thermometer abruptly. He crossed the deck, took the slender glass rod between his thumb and forefinger, and then looked at it carefully.

"Boy," he said. "Boy."

"What is it?"

"A hundred and two point eight," Connerly said. "I guess you really are sick."

"You think I'd snow you?"

"I guess not. We'll get you over to the hospital. It's probably cat fever or some damn thing."

"The hospital again," he complained. "Jesus, a man can't—"

"Second class!" Connerly said, still not able to believe

it. "And a leave in two weeks." He paused and turned suddenly. "Hey, how'd you make out?"

"All right. Listen, if I'm going to the hospital, let's get started. I feel like hell."

"Sure. Sure. I'll talk to the Chief. You can walk, can't you? I mean, we don't need a stretcher or an ambulance?"

"Go talk to the Chief," he said.

That evening, on his way to the quarter-deck and his date with Jean Dvorak, Masters passed through the midships passageway. He saw the posted lists standing side by side on the bulletin board, and he went over for a closer look. His eyes scanned first one list and then the other.

Jones had made radarman second class. He nodded, remembering approving the promotion a long while ago. He looked for Daniels' name on the promotion sheet. It was not there. The yeoman had not advanced.

On the leave schedule, Daniels was up for a leave in three weeks.

Jones's name was not on the leave schedule at all.

8

THERE WAS A MOON THAT NIGHT, AND IT PUT LONG YEL-
low fingers of wavering light on the waters of Chesapeake
Bay. They stood at the rail of the boat, looking out over
the water, hearing the gentle lapping of the waves against
the sides of the boat, hearing the sullen *swish-swish* of the
old-fashioned paddle wheels in their circular housings.

"This is what I call a real busman's holiday," Masters
said.

"It's very nice, though," Jean said. "It's better than a
stuffy old movie, isn't it?"

"Immeasurably," Masters agreed. "Moonlight be-
comes you."

"From the song of the same name," she said.

"Yes, isn't it terrible the way popular songs have made
clichés of sincere sentiments? Oh, well."

They were silent for several moments, watching the
moonlight, listening to the water.

"How'd you drift into the Navy, Jean?" he asked.

"I thought we weren't going to discuss the Navy tonight," she said.

"How'd you drift into the unmentionable?" he asked.

"You sound like Hemingway."

"Why, thanks. But how?"

"I liked nursing. And the Navy needed nurses. So here
I am."

"In Norfolk." Masters shook his head sadly. "They
should have sent you to a better town."

"Norfolk isn't bad," she said.

"No, but it isn't good. That's the big difference." He paused. "Of course, I'm glad they sent you to Norfolk."

"You are?"

"I wouldn't have met you if they hadn't sent you here." He saw her embarrassment and added, "I'm sorry. I keep forgetting that compliments fluster you."

"No, it isn't that," she said.

"What then?"

"Nothing." She lifted her eyes suddenly. "How'd *you* get into the Navy, Chuck?"

"I thought *all* red-blooded American boys went into the Navy sooner or later."

"No, seriously."

"I think I had some idea that it was a worthwhile career," he said.

"And you don't have that idea any more?"

"I'm not sure any more," he said seriously. "Not after what happened with—"

"Ah-ah," she cautioned. "No talking about that, remember?"

"Oh, sure," he said. "Sorry."

"Do you really feel an injustice was done?" she asked after a moment.

"I thought we weren't going to talk about it."

"Why does it bother you so much, Chuck?"

"I don't know. I guess I'm schizophrenic. One half of me says 'Forget it.' The other half says, 'Two people were killed, and the murderer's loose.' Which half am I supposed to listen to?"

"Do you really believe Schaefer's death was a murder?"

"Yes."

"And you still think one of those two men did it? What were their names?"

"Daniels and Jones. Perry Daniels and Alfred Jones."

"You think one of them is guilty?"

"Yes."

"I mean, there's no doubt in your mind? You really believe this?"

"Yes."

"Then follow it through," she said.

"It's going to be a little tough to do that," he said. "I'm leaving for New Jersey in the morning."

"Oh?"

"Radar school," he said.

"Oh," she said again, disappointed.

"And the Old Man's on my back to forget it, and the Exec, and oh, what the hell's the use of shoveling manure against the tide? Why don't I just let it rest? Except . . . except . . ."

"What, Chuck?"

"Did Claire ever mention anything about her secret date being a married man?"

"Married? No, not that I can remember. Why?"

"Well, Perry Daniels is married, according to his records. He told me he was single. Now, why the hell would he do that, unless he had something to conceal? I mean, it adds a new reason for keeping the whole thing secret—aside from the obvious officer-enlisted-man angle. You see, it might provide a possible motive. A married man has much more to lose than a single man. I mean, if his sweetheart suddenly decided to get balky. Do you see what I'm driving at?"

"Yes, of course. But she never mentioned anything about it. Not that I can remember."

"She probably wouldn't have, even if she knew. And maybe she didn't know. Or maybe she didn't know, and then she found out—which strengthens the motive." He paused. "Or maybe I'm all wet."

"No, everything you say sounds possible."

"Sure, but how do you go about . . . Oh, why don't I shut up and kiss you?"

"I've been wondering," she said softly, and then she went into his arms.

* * *

He was familiar with the hospital routine. Connerly brought him to the entry desk, and a pharmacist's mate there took his name, rank, and serial number. Connerly gave him all the pertinent information dully, a matter of routine.

He turned then to his shipmate. "O.K., pal," he said. "Get well quick, as the civilians say."

"Thanks."

Connerly left, and the pharmacist's mate eyed the man from the *Sykes* and said, "Want to follow me? Take your pea coat and your ditty bag."

He followed the pharmacist's mate to a room at the end of the corridor. "You can put your coat in there, mate."

"Won't someone steal it?" he asked.

The pharmacist's mate shrugged. "What's the matter? Don't you trust us?"

"I don't trust anyone," he answered.

"Well, you got to put it in there, anyway. Those are the regulations."

"You know what you can do with regulations, don't you?"

"Look, Mac . . ."

"All right, all right," he said. He took his pea coat into the room and hung it on a hook alongside the other blue jackets.

"We'll get you some pajamas," the pharmacist's mate said. "Come on, follow me."

He followed the pharmacist's mate down the antiseptic-smelling corridors of the hospital. They stopped at another room, and a second pharmacist's mate looked up from a copy of *Married Love,* put the book down, and handed a pair of pajamas and a towel over the counter top.

"You better go to the head before I show you your bed," the first pharmacist's mate said. "You'll be on bedpan after this. What's wrong with you, anyway?"

"Cat fever, they said."

The pharmacist's mate shrugged. "You can change your

clothes in the head, too. You got any valuables you want checked?''

''I'll keep them with me, thanks.''

''That's right. You don't trust nobody.''

''Not even my mother, mate.''

''That's a bad way to be, mate. I feel for you.''

He smiled and left the pharmacist's mate. In the head, he put on the pajamas and then put his wallet into his ditty bag, in which he had packed his toilet articles and his stationery. When he came outside again, the pharmacist's mate was leaning against the wall.

''This way,'' he said. ''You give me them clothes and I'll have them checked for you. Ain't no one going to steal your dungarees.''

''How long you been in the Navy, mate?''

''Why?''

''I've had everything from civvy shorts to shoelaces stolen from me.''

''Well, this is a hospital. We take pity on the sick.''

''I know a guy who had a set of dress blues stolen from him while he was flat on his ass with pneumonia.''

''You got pneumonia?''

''No.''

''Then stop worrying. Here's your bed.''

He looked through the doorway. ''A private room?'' he asked happily.

''Yeah. You really rate.''

''How come?''

''The ward is jammed. Besides, this room was just vacated.'' The pharmacist's mate paused. ''The guy who had it suddenly dropped dead.''

''Oh.''

''Damn'est thing you ever saw,'' the pharmacist's mate continued. ''Comes in with a simple thing, and all of a sudden drops dead.''

''What'd he come in with?''

''Cat fever,'' the pharmacist's mate said sourly. ''Sleep tight, mate.''

He went into the room smiling. He had not expected a private room, and the unforeseen windfall worked like a shot in the arm. He hung his ditty bag on the bedpost, taking his wallet from it and stuffing it between the pillow and the pillowcase. He tested the mattress with his palm, pleased with the soft comfort of it, pleased with the crisp white sheets. This was a far cry from the sack aboard ship. Ah, yes, there was nothing like hospital duty. Bull's-eyes and toast tomorrow morning, orange juice. Ah, this was grand.

He pulled back the covers and climbed into bed.

He'd have to act sick in the beginning, of course. He'd really had cat fever once, and so he knew the symptoms he was supposed to show. It wouldn't do to be suspected of malingering. He'd irritate his throat by chewing on some tobacco shreds, and this was as good a time as any to do that. He reached into his ditty bag, pulled out a package of cigarettes, and then broke one of the cigarettes open, aware of the fact that nicotine was a poison, but not planning on chewing that much of it. He put several shreds on his tongue, wincing when the bitterness filled his mouth. He forced them to the back of his throat, almost choking on them, and then he spat them onto the palm of his hand.

He began clearing his throat, purposely straining it, wanting red to show when the doctors examined him. He didn't know how he'd raise his temperature again, but he'd figure something. A lighted cigarette in the ash tray, perhaps, and then some subterfuge to get the nurse out of the room. He'd work it. He'd worked it before, and there was no reason to think he couldn't work it this time.

He was very pleased with the way things were going. He'd been spotted by Schaefer last time, but that was on a ward. He had a private room to himself this time, and that meant he'd be alone with whatever nurse they gave him. He had very rarely met any woman who hadn't appealed to him in some way, so he wasn't anticipating a nurse he couldn't stomach. Women were very funny that way. If they had ugly phizzes, they generally had good

bodies and vice versa. Claire had been exceptional in that
she was pretty and also owned a body like a brick—Well,
there was no sense thinking about her any more. Besides, even if he did draw a dog, he could die for Old
Glory. The punch line amused him. He sat in bed, smiling, anticipating his first encounter with whatever nurse
they gave him.

He had to admit that he was very clever.

Oh, sure, there were sluts in Norfolk. Christ knew there
were a million sluts in Norfolk, but the day he had to pay
for it, that was the day he'd hand in his jock. And there
were Waves on the base, too, but the Waves were always
surrounded by enlisted men, and you had to fight off ten
guys before you got near one.

Nurses were the ticket, all right. Sure, nurses were officers, and as such were strictly reserved for other officers.
That was a stupid rule, all right, that nonfraternization
thing. That's a rule against human nature, by Jesus! What
is a man supposed to do? Can a man help it if he's got a
normal human appetite? Hell, no, of course he can't. But
try to tell that to the brass, just try to explain that to them.

Well, he was very clever about it all. And he was sure
enough of his charm to know that once he got to meet a
girl, the rest was in the bag. Sometimes he figured his
being an enlisted man was in his favor. There was something pretty exciting about doing something that was for-
bidden. Like a stolen apple tasting better, that kind of
thing. The nurses could get all the officers they wanted,
but he guessed there was something dull about that. This
way, there was an element of danger involved, and any
girl liked that element of danger.

"Hi," a voice said from the doorway.

He looked up, seeing the pharmacist's mate again.

"Hi," he answered.

"Got a chart for you," the pharmacist's mate said.
"How you feeling?"

"Lousy."

"You don't look so lousy."

"No? What's that got to do with the way I feel?"

"Nothing. I just don't trust people.'Specially people with cat fever."

"You the doctor here?"

"Nope."

"Then it ain't your job to diagnose. Besides, I'm the distrustful guy, remember?"

"Sure. I remember." The pharmacist's mate went to the foot of the bed and clipped the fresh chart there. "You been here before, ain't you?"

"Yeah," he said slowly.

"I thought I recognized you."

"So?"

"So nothing. You're a sickly type, I guess."

"That's right, I'm a sickly type."

"Mmm," the pharmacist's mate said, nodding. "When's the doctor coming around?"

"You can relax," the pharmacist's mate said. "He's made his last rounds for today. He won't be around again till tomorrow morning. Not unless you're dropping dead. Are you dropping dead?"

"No," he answered.

"I didn't figure. I heard you choking a while back, though, so I figured maybe you was ready to kick off. You want me to get the doc, I'll be happy to do that for you."

"I can wait until morning."

The pharmacist's mate smiled. "Don't I know it," he said.

"If you're finished piddling around, I'd like to get some rest."

"Sure," the pharmacist's mate said, smiling. "Got to let a sick man get his rest. Had to give you a chart, though, you understand that, don't you? Can't tell the sick ones from the fakers without a chart."

"Are you looking for trouble, mate?" he asked suddenly.

"Me? Perish the thought."

"Then get the hell of my back."

"Sure." He shook his head. "You sure talk tough for a sick man."

"I'm not so sick that I can't—"

"G'night, mate. Sleep tight."

The pharmacist's mate left the room, and he watched the broad back in the undress blues jumper turn outside the door and vanish. He cursed the bastard, and then leaned back against the pillow, wondering if the pecker checker would cause him any trouble. All he needed was a malingering charge against him. That would mean a captain's mast, sure as hell. If not a deck court. Goddamnit, why'd people have to stick their noses into your business?

When he heard footsteps again, he thought it was the pharmacist's mate returning, and then he recognized the hushed whisper of the hospital slippers that were generally handed out to ambulatory cases.

A boy poked his head around the doorjamb tentatively.

He was a tall boy with brown hair and blue eyes, a kid of no more than eighteen or nineteen. He wore the faded blue hospital robe and the fabric slippers, and his face was very pale, as if he'd been isolated from the sun for a long time.

"You just check in?" he asked.

"Yes."

"My name's Guibert. You sick?"

"I'm in the hospital, ain't I?"

Guibert entered the room. "Mind if I come in?"

"Well . . ."

"I'm the official welcoming committee. I been here for eight months now. I see everybody who comes and goes. Guibert the Greeter, they call me. Ain't I seen you around before?"

"Maybe," he answered. Goddamnit, was the whole hospital full of spies?

"What's your name?" Guibert asked.

"What difference does it make?"

"I just like to know."

"It's on the chart," he said frostily.

Guibert looked briefly at the chart. "What's wrong with you?"

"Cat fever."

"You're lucky."

"Am I?"

"Sure," Guibert said. "I been here for eight months now, like I told you, and they still don't know what's wrong with me."

"Yeah?" he said dubiously.

"God's truth, s'help me. I been looked over by every doctor in the Navy practically." Guibert shrugged. "They can't figure it out."

"Are you contagious?" he asked suddenly.

"Me? No, don't worry about that. They thought so in the beginning, but no more now. They had me isolated for three months, figuring I was carrying a dread disease or something. But I ain't. They just don't know what I got."

"That right?" he asked, interested now.

"Yeah," Guibert said sadly. "I just run a fever all the time. A hun' one, a hun' two, like that. Never goes no higher. But it's always there, day and night. Man, a fever like that can drain you, you know it?"

"I can imagine," he said. "And you been here eight months?"

"Eight months and six days, you want to be exact about it. The doctors think I got bit by a bug or something. I was in the Pacific before I come here, on the *Coral Sea*. They think I got bit by some rare tropical bug. Man, I got a disease unknown to medical science. How's that for an honor?"

"Nobody else has this disease?" he asked.

Guibert shook his head, a little proudly, a little in awe. "Not that they know of. How's that for something? You know, they thought I was goofin' off at first. Malingering, you know? But they couldn't pass off the thermometer readings. Every damn day, a hun' one, a hun' two. Puzzled the hell out of them.

"So they finally sent me over to see a psychiatrist. He give me that Rorschach test, and a lot of other tests, puttin' arms and legs on a torso, and fittin' pegs into holes, things like that. They even give me an electroencephalograph test. You ever hear of that?"

"No," he said.

"Yeah, it's a test measures brain waves. They put these little wires on your skull, like they're gonna electrocute you or something, and this measures your brain waves. They can tell from that whether you got a illness or not, like a tumor or something, you know? Well, I ain't got nothing like that. My brain waves are perfectly O.K. And the psychiatrist says he never saw nobody as normal as me. Which is why they are all so puzzled. If I ain't goofing, and if I ain't nuts, then what's wrong with me?"

"Search me," he said.

"Sometimes I wonder myself. I never got bit by no bug, I can swear to that. There was a lot of bugs on Guam, but I never got bit. So how come I run this fever all the time? The way I got it figured, I'll be in this damn hospital for the rest of my life!"

"Do they give you liberty?"

"No. Hell, no, how can they do that? I'm a walking guinea pig. They find out what's wrong with me, man, they can lick cancer and the common cold." Guibert shook his head sadly.

"Well, it can't be too bad here."

"Oh, no, it ain't bad at all. Bunch of nice guys, and some real doll nurses. We got a honey on this floor, wait'll you meet her. We got four of them, you know, but this one is a real peach. A nice girl."

"Yeah?" he asked, interested again.

"Yeah, you'll see her. Hey, are you from Brooklyn?"

"No."

"Oh. That's a shame. I'm from Brooklyn. I keep asking guys where they're from, like in boot camp. When you can't get out, you're anxious to meet guys from your neighborhood, you know?"

"Yes," he said.

"What ship you off?"

"U.S.S. *Sykes,*" he said.

"What's that?"

"A tin can."

"That's good duty, ain't it?"

"Well, it's not bad," he said.

"The *Sykes,*" Guibert said. "That sounds familiar. Why should it sound familiar?"

"I don't know," he answered, shrugging.

Guibert thought about it for a moment, and then he shrugged, too. "Well, no matter."

"This nurse . . ." he started.

"I'm a fire-control man, you know that?" Guibert said.

"No, I didn't know."

"Yeah. Went to school for it. You been on a carrier?"

"No."

"What's your rate?" Guibert asked.

"I'm a—"

"This is a sick man we got here, Guibert," a voice from the doorway said.

He turned his head. The pharmacist's mate was back again.

"Oh, I'm sorry," Guibert said. "I didn't realize it, Greg."

"Yeah, he's very sick," the pharmacist's mate said. "Very, very sick."

"Well, then, I'll be running along, Greg."

"I think you'd better," Greg said.

"Nice meeting you, mate," Guibert said.

"Same here," he answered.

Greg looked at him, and then smiled broadly. "You better get that rest you need. The doc'll be around in the morning."

He smiled back at Greg. "Sure," he said. And he thought, And the nurses, too. The nurses, too.

9

SHE STOOD BEFORE THE FULL-LENGTH MIRROR IN HER
room, not wanting to awaken her roommate and not yet
wanting to go to bed.

She looked at herself as if she were meeting the reflection for the first time, and she felt rather idiotic about the
sudden bursting feeling within her.

She had never met anyone like Chuck Masters before,
never in all her life.

She'd been born on a farm in Minnesota, the proverbial
farmer's daughter, except that her father was a strict, God-
fearing man who wouldn't have allowed a salesman within
four acres of his property. She could still remember the
wheat fields, even now far away from them, the slender
rods of grain swaying on the afternoon breeze, the sky a
solid mass of blue beyond it, the sun glaring in the sky
overhead. She had loved to walk in the wheat when she
was a young girl, her head almost covered by the swaying
golden wands.

She was a quiet, introverted child, Jean Dvorak. She
loved the farm animals, and her favorite stories were those
in which animals figured largely. She had never liked boys
much. There was a nice boy living on the neighboring
farm, a boy called Sven. He would often come to visit
with his father, and he'd hop down from the wagon and
they would race over the fields together, barefoot, laughing at the sun. This was when they were both very young,
before she fully realized there was a difference between
boys and girls.

When she was twelve, and her breasts began to pucker

with adolescence, her mother explained what was happening to her. She could still remember her mother quite
clearly, her hair as golden as the wheat fields, her eyes as
blue as the sky beyond. Her mother was a gentle woman
who put up with the harsh ways of her father patiently,
and she remembered now the extreme sense of loss she'd
felt when her mother died. They had laid her to rest in the
rich Minnesota earth, and she had wept silently, and her
heart had gone out then to the woman who had been her
friend all her life.

She had three brothers and no sisters, and with her mother gone, there was no one to tell her things any more.
Sven would still come over with his father, but he had
begun to notice her as a girl now, and when he leaped
down from the wagon bed, he would stand around and
foolishly worry the ground with his big toe.

She preferred her books to Sven.

She went on to high school, and she was considered a
quiet, studious girl. She was asked to join a sorority, but
she refused. She was asked out often, but she rarely ac-
cepted dates, even though the boys never stopped trying.
There was something exceptionally appealing about her
dignified good looks, and she could have been the belle
of the school had she tried, but she did not try.

Her mother had died of cancer, and the cruel injustice
of her death had remained with Jean for a long while afterward. She wanted to do something to help. Her father
was not a rich man, and so she abandoned any hope of
becoming a doctor. But nursing was a worthwhile profession, and she discussed it with the student adviser at
school, who suggested that she go into the Navy upon
graduation.

She had been a good student, and she was a good nurse,
highly respected at the hospital.

This thing with Chuck—she could not fool herself about
this thing with Chuck. He was the first man who'd really
captured her interest, but she wondered now if she were

really in love with him, or if she were simply experiencing something she should have felt when she was fifteen.

She looked at herself in the mirror again, and then she began undressing, taking off her jacket and then her hat. He was not really a handsome man. She had met handsomer men, and they had all left her cold. Nor was he more intelligent than most, or more sincere, or more trustworthy, or more anything, for that matter. He had simply appealed to her, and he still appealed to her, and that was the long and the short of it, she supposed.

She took off her blouse and her skirt, and then went back to the mirror, standing in her bra and half-slip.

She supposed she was an attractive woman. Her bust was as good as most she'd seen—and God, she'd seen enough of them since she'd entered the Navy—and whereas she was a little hippy, she supposed her figure would do. Chuck seemed to like it, anyway. Or so she imagined.

That was the danger of a thing like this, the fact that a girl could let her imagination run away with her. She had met a lot of men in the Navy, and every man she'd met seemed to feel her nurse's uniform was a symbol of promiscuity, or at least a promise of it. She really couldn't understand this. She had heard stories about Waves, of course, and she had also heard stories about her sister nurses, but a uniform didn't necessarily make its wearer a loose woman. She was, in fact, willing to wager that the uniform had nothing whatever to do with it. Those same girls would undoubtedly have behaved in the same manner in civilian dress. Claire, for example. Well, there was no sense thinking about Claire, God rest her soul.

The important person to think about was Chuck.

Was it possible that he was like all the rest? He had, after all, asked her out the moment he'd met her, practically, and that hardly spoke well for an enduring friendship. And the second time he'd met her, he'd been drunk, and he'd probably have settled for anything in a skirt.

She had been quite carried away with him that second time. There had been something immensely attractive about him, and she couldn't quite put her finger on what it was. Perhaps a stilted sort of mother complex, a protection of the poor drunk. But that didn't explain her reaction to his kisses. No mother ever felt that way about her child.

Now let us draw up the reins, Miss Dvorak, she warned herself. This may just be a grand little fling for the good lieutenant, and if it is, he's going to be sadly disappointed. It doesn't seem as if he feels that way, but there's really no way of telling. Not yet, there isn't. And he has been a perfect gentleman, except for his kisses. No perfect gentleman kisses that way.

So let's just take it easy. He'll be in New Jersey for a while. Now, where in New Jersey? He didn't even tell me, which shows how much he cares, but he did promise to write. What more can you expect of a fellow?

Still, and nonetheless, I really honestly feel we should bide our time and step forward cautiously. We've already exhibited our heart on our striped sleeve, and that was the wrong thing to do at this stage of the game.

Perhaps I should get to know some other men.

Perhaps I should go out more often. What's wrong with me, anyway, falling like a silly adolescent for the first man that comes my way!

I'll go with other men.

Well, maybe I won't. Chuck will only be gone for a short time, and he did say he'd write, though maybe he won't. We'll see, I suppose, and besides, who'd ask me out if he doesn't?

Well, that's silly. You're certainly asked out often enough, so don't make excuses for the Lieutenant. You know darned well you're crazy about him already, so don't tell yourself . . . Well, why not? What's wrong with going out with some other men while he's gone? Am I engaged to him or something? Am I married?

Mrs. Charles Masters.

Oh, wouldn't that be lovely?

Go to sleep, you silly little fool, she told herself, and then she whipped off her underclothes and headed for her bed.

10

"You can call me Greg," the pharmacist's mate
said. "All my friends call me Greg."

"Thanks," he answered.

"And I want you to consider yourself my buddy, mate.
I really want you to consider yourself my buddy."

He stared at Greg curiously. The pharmacist's mate was
driving at something, he was sure of that. He didn't know
what, though, and his uncertainty displeased him.

"It never hurts to have buddies," he said.

"No, it don't, and that's a fact," Greg answered. "Especially when they're on a hospital ward, eh, buddy?"

"What do you mean?"

"Oh, nothing," Greg said. He paused. "You passed
sick call this morning, didn't you?"

"I didn't know I was taking an exam," he said.

"Ah, but you were. Now come on, mate. You knew
you were taking a big test, didn't you? You must have
known that."

"I don't follow."

"How do you like Miss Piel?"

"Who?"

"Your nurse," Greg said. "The one come around with
Dr. Melville."

"She was all right."

"Nice piece, wouldn't you say?"

"So-so," he answered.

"You didn't look so-so, mate. You looked like you was
gonna eat her up. What's the matter? Ain't there no women
on your ship?" Greg burst out laughing. "Yeah, she's a

105

peacheroo, Miss Piel. Only thing, she's engaged to a full commander. Now, that's a damn shame, ain't it?''

"Doesn't bother me one way or the other,'' he said.

"It don't? Well, now, that's mighty interesting to hear. Especially after the way your eyes was popping out of your head when she stuck that thermometer in your mouth. How'd you swing a fever, mate? A hundred and one, the chart reads. How'd you do it?''

"I'm a sick man,'' he said.

"Sure, no question about it. I'll bet you're even sicker after what I told you about Miss Piel.''

"What're you driving at, Greg?''

"Me? Hell, mate, I'm not driving at anything. I just notice you got an eye for the broads, that's all. Nothing wrong with that, is there?''

"Nothing at all,'' he answered tightly.

"Give you a few tips, in fact. Miss Lemmon, she's on night duty tonight. Not a very pretty wench, but very dedicated to her profession. Hates to see anyone suffer. Tell her you're burning up with fever, and she'll give you an alcohol rub. She's got very gentle hands, Miss Lemmon.'' Greg was smiling broadly. "That appeal to you, mate?''

"What's your game, Greg?''

"What's yours?'' Greg asked point-blank.

"I've got cat fever. That's no game.''

"You're not sore at me, are you mate? After all the tips I'm giving you?''

"I don't need any tips. I'm sick, and that's it.''

"You're sick like I'm sick.''

"Blow,'' he said suddenly. "Get the hell out of here, Greg.''

"Sure. One more tip, though. Watch for the nurse comes on at twelve hundred. Now, she is really something, mate. Really something you should go for. And we do want to make your stay here a pleasant one, now don't we?''

"I'm not looking for any nurses,'' he said.

"No?'' Greg's eyes narrowed. "I remember you, mate.

Maybe you was too busy to notice me the last time you was here, but I remember you. I remember you goddamn well. I got a memory like an elephant.''

"Yeah?"

"Yeah," Greg said tersely.

"So?"

"Nothing. Just remember that I remember you." He walked to the door. "I'll be seeing you, mate."

"Not if I see you first," he called after Greg.

At 1223, Jean Dvorak walked into his room.

"Hello," she said. "I'm Miss Dvorak." She smiled professionally. "And how are you feeling today?"

"Pretty miserable," he said, his eyes lighting. Greg hadn't lied to him. This one was really something. This one made all the others look sick. This one was for him.

"Oh, really? Well, now let's see." She walked to the foot of the bed and lifted his chart, her eye passing rapidly over his name and then dropping to the temperature recordings.

"I got cat fever," he said.

"Yes, I see that. Well, your temperature hasn't been too high." She smiled again. "I think you'll survive."

"I'm *sure* I will," he said. "Now that I've got something to live for."

She looked at him curiously for a moment, and then she gave a tiny shrug. "You get all the rest you can," she said.

"How does it feel?" he asked.

"How does what feel?"

"Being an ensign?"

"I never much think about it," Jean said.

"Don't you feel sort of silly when an enlisted man salutes you?"

She smiled and said, "As a matter of fact, I do."

"I thought so."

"Why'd you think so?"

"I don't know. I just figured you for the kind of girl a uniform didn't mean very much to. The stripe, I mean."

"Mmm. Well, you're very observant."

"I try to be."

"You're also very talkative. You should be getting some sleep."

"I'm not sleepy. Not any more."

"Aren't you? Well. Perhaps I'd best call the doctor and have you released. If you feel that well, I mean."

"I'm still pretty sick," he said, smiling.

She went to the bed and put her hand on his forehead.

"My mother used to do that," he said.

"You don't feel very warm."

"I think maybe the fever is dropping. It's supposed to drop after a while, isn't it?"

"Yes. Well, we'll see."

She started from the bed, and he said, "Are you going so soon?"

"Why, yes," she said, surprised.

"Why don't you come back again? Later."

She looked at him, her mouth and eyes curling in amused surprise. "What for?"

"We'll . . . talk a little."

"Well, maybe," she said.

"It'll help me get better," he added hastily. "I've been very lonely."

"Lonely? You were just admitted last night."

"I know. But I get lonely in hospitals."

"Well, I've got to see my other patients."

"And afterward, will you come back?"

"You're a persistent young man, aren't you?"

"I'm just lonely," he said.

"I'll see."

"Promise."

"Now, really . . ."

"Or don't you talk to enlisted men?"

"Whatever gave you that idea?"

"Navy Regs," he said.

"I don't think Navy Regs apply to a nurse talking to her patient," Jean said.

"Then you *will* be back?"

"I didn't say that. You're something of a seagoing lawyer, aren't you?"

"Come on, Miss Dvorak," he said. "Say you'll come back."

"I'm overwhelmed," she said, smiling and shaking her head. "You get some sleep now."

"I'll see you later?"

"I might stop by. If I'm not too busy."

"Promise," he said.

"I never make promises I'm not sure I'll keep."

"Then promise, and keep the promise."

"They ought to make you a recruiting officer," she said.

"Then you'll come back?"

"Yes, later. For just a few minutes."

"I'll be waiting."

"Breathlessly, no doubt," she said, and left the room.

She went back to him a little later, after she'd seen her other patients. He was propped up in bed, the pillow behind him, and he stared through the window, with the sun laying long golden bars across his face. He looked very weak and very pathetic that way, and she paused in the doorway for a moment before entering. She had always felt an enormous sympathy for anyone who was ill, and his pose when she entered was such a desolately lonely one that she felt a sudden wrench of her heart. He kept staring through the window, unaware of her presence, and she wondered for a moment if she shouldn't leave him with his thoughts. Instead, she walked crisply to the foot of his bed, and he turned when he heard the rustle of her uniform, and then a smile mushroomed on his face.

"Hi," he said. "I thought you weren't coming."

"I promised, didn't I?"

"Yes, you did. Gee, I'm glad to see you."

"I hope I didn't interrupt anything. You looked so . . . so solemn."

Pain seemed to stab his eyes, and he turned his head for a moment, the sun limning his profile. "Well, you know," he said.

"No, I don't. Is something wrong?"

He turned to face her again, studying her, studying her minutely, as if trying to memorize her features. "No, nothing," he said at last. He smiled broadly. "Nothing to worry your pretty head about, anyway."

Jean looked at him curiously. "If it's anything I can help with . . ."

"No, no, nothing. It's just . . . a fellow gets lonely sometimes."

"How long have you been in the Navy?" Jean asked.

"Oh, awhile."

"Homesick?"

"A little."

She raised her brows and looked at him again. There was a strange quality about him, a feeling of utter truth that was somehow submerged. She couldn't tell whether or not he was being honest with her, or whether his tongue was in his cheek, and this inability to determine his motives annoyed her and piqued her interest at the same time. For no real reason, she asked, "Are you married?"

"No," he answered quickly, without hesitation.

"Girl back home?"

"No," he said. "That's not it."

"Just miss things in general, is that it? Your town, the people there?"

"I suppose," he said, and his voice was lonely and forlorn again, and she felt once more an enormous sympathy sweeping over her.

"I feel like that sometimes, too," she said. "It's a normal thing." She paused. "It's hard to pick up your roots. The Navy asks you to do that, but it's very hard, I know."

"Do you like the Navy, Miss Dvorak?" he asked.

"Yes. Very much."

"Good." He paused. "I do, too."

"Well, good. That makes two of us."

"Except . . . well, never mind."

"No, what is it?" she asked.

"Well, the regulations. Sometimes they bother me."

"The regulations bother everyone. You have to have regulations, or you wouldn't have a navy."

"Oh, don't misunderstand me, Jean—" He cut himself short. "Say, is it all right to call you Jean?"

"Well . . ."

"See, that's what I mean about regulations. Isn't it natural for a guy and a girl to call each other by their first names? Well, sure it is. But I have to be careful about calling you Jean. Now that's silly, isn't it?"

"Well . . ." She smiled. "I guess it is silly, when you consider it."

"May I call you Jean?"

She hesitated. "I don't think so."

"Why not?"

"Well, regulations . . ."

"Sure," he said, the sadness back in his voice again.

"Oh, now don't look so desolate."

"No, it's all right."

"Really, it's not that important."

"It *is* important to me," he said. His eyes sought hers. "It's very important that I call you Jean."

"Well, if it's that important . . ." She smiled mischievously. "Suppose you call me Jean, then. But only in this room, all right?"

"And will you call me by my first name?"

"I don't even know your first name," she said. "In fact, I'm not even sure of your last name."

"You're kidding me. I thought surely you'd memorized the chart by now."

"No, I'm afraid I haven't," she said, still smiling. "In fact, I have a confession. To me, you're just One-o-seven."

"One-o-seven?"

"The room number," she said, gesturing toward the door with her head.

"One-o-seven," he repeated, wagging his head. "The Navy's finally reduced me to a cipher. Look, will you do me a favor?"

"That depends."

"You won't even have to look at the chart, how's that? I mean, I'll make it real easy for you, no fuss, no muss. O.K.?"

"It still depends."

"I'll give you my name. No work involved. No walking around to the foot of the bed, no eyestrain. How about it? All you have to do is promise you'll call me by it."

She thought about this for several moments. Then she said, "No."

"Why not?" he said plaintively.

"It's better this way." She nodded her head. "It's better if you remain One-o-seven."

He looked crestfallen. "You engaged or something?"

"No," she said slowly.

"Going steady?"

"No."

"A guy?"

"Maybe a guy," she admitted.

"Would he object to your calling me by my first name? Gee, is that a lot to ask? It's not as if I'm . . . Well, I'm only asking you to . . ." He spread his hands in frustration.

"One-o-seven," she said again, smiling.

"Well, I guess I know when I'm licked. That's a nice name when you get down to it, I suppose. Has a good ring, and it's sure individual. Oh, yes. I knew a guy named One-o-eight once, but I never met anybody named One-o-seven."

She burst out laughing and then stopped abruptly, still unable to keep the smile off her face.

"You're really very beautiful when you smile, did you know that?" he asked.

His statement surprised her, and her thoughts fled back to that night in the Officers' Club, when Chuck had used almost the exact words. She thought of Chuck now, and a blush rose on her throat, spread into her face.

"I'm sorry," he said. "I didn't mean to embarrass you, Jean."

"It's just . . . never mind. Thank you for your compliment."

"With love, from One-o-seven," he said, smiling.

She rose abruptly, glancing at her watch. "I've got to go. This has been very nice."

"I enjoyed it," he said. "Will you come back again?"

"Oh, you'll see me around. You'll get to hate me."

His face grew suddenly serious. "I'll never get to hate you, Jean," he said, and his eyes were so penetrating that she knew she would blush again unless she got out of the room immediately.

"Get some sleep," she said, and then she whirled on her heel and walked out of the room.

From the end of the corridor, Greg saw her leaving 107. His eyes followed her until she rounded the bend in the corridor, and then he turned back to the report he was filling out, annoyed when he found his concentration had been destroyed.

What was it about that bastard in 107? What was it?

Something, that was for sure. Something you just sensed. When you'd been around hospitals long enough, you automatically knew who was goofing off and who was really sick. And 107 was goofing, Greg would bet his bottom dollar on that.

Cat fever, the old standby. Don't know what else to call it? Cat fever. Greg was even willing to bet they'd diagnosed poor Guibert as cat fever when he first came aboard. So 107 was pulling a switch on the old routine. He was a shrewd bastard, all right, no getting away from that. He was shrewd, and the shrewdness annoyed the hell out of Greg, especially now, especially after he'd seen Miss Dvorak leaving the room. She'd been in there for close to twenty minutes, and that's too long for any nurse to spend with any patient, especially an innocent doll like Miss Dvorak and especially with a shrewd bastard like 107.

What was his game? That was the big question, all right. The guy in 107 had a game, as sure as God made little green apples. Just malingering? Yeah, maybe. Was he bucking for a medical discharge? No, he'd have chosen something stronger than cat fever if that's what he was up to. So what then? Maybe he was going to pull a psycho routine, maybe that was it. Start foaming at the mouth, falling down on the floor, brushing bedbugs off him, things like that. Well, don't brush them on me, pal.

Damnit, why don't I like the poor sonofabitch? Greg wondered. He may be really sick, when you get down to it.

The hell he is.

O.K., so he ain't sick.

Damn right, he ain't.

Then what's his game?

I don't know, Greg admitted. But I'm sure as hell going to find out!

11

CHUCK MASTERS TRIED TO MAKE HIS HEAD COMFORTABLE
against the coarsely padded back of the seat.

In all his experience with trains, he had never achieved
that simple goal of making himself comfortable, and this
experience, he silently reflected, was no different from any
of the others. The people who designed trains, he was
sure, were the same people who designed such things as
electric chairs and subterranean torture chambers. If you
put your head this way, he thought, it's no good. And if
you put your head the other way, it's still no good. What
I really need is a Pullman. But he'd been in Pullmans, too,
and he'd never been able to sleep, and oh, hell, he should
have joined the Air Force.

He achieved some measure of comfort, finally, by sort
of twisting his head a little to starboard and tilting it back
slightly just a smidgin, just about maybe three degrees.
He didn't dare move his head because he'd been striving
for this position ever since the train had begun its labori-
ous journey, and he was certainly not one to look a gift
horse in the mouth. Outside the window, he could see the
countryside falling away, the bland Southern sky imper-
ceptibly changing to the harsher, bleaker Northern sky. He
began counting telephone poles. The poles were regularly
spaced, set into the ground at slightly different depths so
that the wires plunged and rose, plunged and rose again.

Jesus, I'm getting seasick.

He turned his attention from the telephone poles and
the scenery beyond the window, and he concentrated on
the window directly before him, in which the aisle and the

115

seats opposite were reflected. A girl was sitting in one of the seats. She was a redhead, and she was wearing a tight green woolen suit and a short topper, and her legs were crossed, and there was a gold ankle bracelet around one ankle. The crossed legs exposed a goodly amount of white, fleshy thigh, and the girl seemed cognizant of this fact, proud of it, for that matter, and for a moment Masters wanted to turn his head from the reflection and enjoy the splendor of the real image. He balanced the desirability of viewing an expanse of thigh against the desirability of keeping the comfortable position he had finally found. And into his reasoning came the coldly logical fact that he was on a Navy mission, and even if the young lady proved to be as interesting as her interesting thigh promised, she'd probably get off the train in Washington, and he'd go on to Atlantic City, and where would that leave him? Of course, there was a portion of night travel ahead, and heaven only knew what could happen on a dimly lighted train speeding through the night with a redhead who looked the way this one did, and who went around flashing comfortably padded white-winking thighs all over the place.

The debate assumed major proportions in his mind. He was an officer of the United States Navy, he reminded himself, and his conduct should become an officer of the United States Navy, but the thigh persistently winked at him in the reflection. The girl had put down her magazine now, and he caught a glimpse of the title. One of the romance magazines, and that too weighed heavily in the young lady's favor. She sucked in a deep breath that threatened the strength of her upper garments, and Masters was almost ready to rise and make the young lady's acquaintance when he thought of Jean Dvorak. At the same time, one of the radarmen walked down the aisle and plopped into the vacant seat beside Masters, so that he never really knew whether it was the radarman or Jean Dvorak who prevented him from getting to meet and perhaps know the redhead with the extroverted thigh.

"Hello, Mr. Masters," the radarman said.

"Hello," Masters answered. He did not turn his head. If a redhead could not budge him from the dubious comfort he had at last achieved, a radarman certainly wasn't going to turn the trick.

"Mind if I sit here?" the radarman asked.

"Go right ahead," Masters said.

The radarman, who was already sitting anyway, made himself comfortable. "Ah, this is nice," he murmured.

Masters wondered about his sanity, until he realized the radarman was sitting directly opposite the redhead, without the slightly smudged hindrance of a reflection in the window.

"Ain't it, sir?" the radarman said.

"The ride, or the scenery?" Masters asked.

"Oh, both, sir. Both."

Masters grunted, not moving his head.

"Very nice," the radarman said, apparently very comfortable in the seat now, apparently planning to spend the night there, or perhaps the rest of the month, or even the rest of his life. "When you think we'll be there, sir?"

"Early in the morning," Masters said.

"Think we'll get liberty?"

"I doubt it."

"Oh."

"I can't see your face," Masters said, "and I don't want to turn."

The radarman looked at him curiously, wondering if the Lieutenant were sick or something.

"Who are you?" Masters asked.

"Me?" the radarman asked back.

"Yes."

"Oh. I'm Caldroni. Hey, don't you know me? Sir?"

"Yes, Caldroni. I know you very well."

"For a minute there—"

"Where are the other men?"

"Oh, all in this car."

"Good."

"Yes, sir." Caldroni was silent for a long while. "Sir?" he whispered at length.

"Mmm?"

"She's something, ain't she, sir?" he whispered.

"The redhead?"

"Yes, sir."

"Yes, she's something."

"Begging your pardon, sir, but is there anything outside that window that is important to our mission, sir? What I mean to say, sir, is that if you are concerned with duty, I can understand your interest. But if you are not, sir, then may I suggest—"

"I am concerned with comfort, Caldroni," Masters said.

"To be sure, sir. Aren't we all?" His voice dropped to a whisper again. "This one is built for comfort, sir."

"Yes, I know."

"Yes, sir." Caldroni glanced at the redhead again. "Sir, have you ever been to Atlantic City?"

"No," Masters said.

"A very nice place, I understand. One of the fellows lives in Jersey. He says Atlantic City is real gone."

"I'm glad to hear that."

"Yes, sir. You think there won't be no liberty at all, sir? None at all?"

"We'll see," Masters said. He paused. "Did the others send you, Caldroni?"

"The others? What others, sir?"

"The men in the radar gang."

"Oh, no, sir. Send me where, sir?"

"Send you here. To find out if there'd be liberty in Atlantic City or not."

"Oh, no, sir. Nossir, sir. Why, whatever put that idea into your head, Mr. Masters?"

"Just an idle thought, Caldroni. Well there may be liberty, we'll see."

"That's very good, sir."

"And now I suppose you'll be leaving my company?"

"Well, sir, if you don't mind—that is, I rather like this seat, you know?" Caldroni looked at the redhead again and wet his lips.

"I see." Masters paused. "Liberty is a funny word, isn't it? It implies imprisonment."

"Sir?"

Masters shrugged. "Another idle thought," he said. "Forget it." He paused again. "What do you do on liberty, Caldroni?"

"Prowl," Caldroni said, smiling.

"Do all the men prowl?"

"Most of 'em, I guess. Unless they're dead. Or married."

Daniels, Masters thought. Perry Daniels. Married.

"Not many married men in our crew, are there, Caldroni?"

"No, not many," Caldroni agreed. "A few, though."

"Do you know Perry Daniels?"

"Oh, yes, sir."

"Well?"

"Very well, sir. I had a personal interest in Daniels at one time. A sort of a professional interest, so to speak. What about him, sir?"

"Is he married?"

"Daniels?" Caldroni chuckled. "Hell, no sir, you'll pardon me."

Masters turned his head, forsaking the comfort he'd attained. "How do you know, Caldroni?"

"Well, it's just a fact, that's all. Daniels ain't married. I mean, you'll forgive me, sir, I think he's a regular ladies' man, you know what I mean?"

"No. What do you mean?"

"Well, sir, when you get aboard a ship, you don't know nobody from a hole in the wall, you know what I mean? A hole in the *bulkhead*, of course." Caldroni seemed embarrassed by his nonnautical slip.

"Yes, go on."

"So you start putting out feelers, you know? First you

find out which of the officers is O.K., and which of them stinks. Present company excluded, naturally.''

"Naturally.''

"A chicken officer can make things tough for you, Mr. Masters, and I ain't casting no aspersions, but the *Sykes* sure got its quota of chicken officers. Present company excluded, naturally.''

"Naturally. Go on.''

"So you learn which officers you can live with, and which officers you wished was dead, and you avoid the ones you can't get along with. You see them strolling down the deck, you cut into a passageway, you follow? In a ship's politics, you got to know which politicians can do the most for you. It's like making a choice—you belong to either the Republican Club or the Democratic Club. O.K., so it's the officers first, because they're most important in making your life comfortable. Then you start looking around and figuring which of the enlisted men you want to buddy with.''

"I see.''

"We're lucky 'cause the radar gang is a nice bunch of guys. But like I said, that's lucky. They could've been a bunch of lemons, and then I'd have been up the creek without a paddle. I didn't take no chances, anyway. When I come aboard, I started making my own private inquiries.''

"What's all this got to do with Perry Daniels?''

"Well, sir, you got to choose who you want on liberty, you follow? You don't want a slob, and you don't want a guy's too eager, and at the same time you don't want some jerk doesn't know how to part his hair right, you see? If you're going to prowl, you got to choose a good prowling mate. New, Singer is just about the best prowling mate a buddy could have. Now, he really knows how to approach a girl. You can put Singer ashore in any town in the world, and I can guarantee—''

"But what about Daniels?''

"Daniels? He's got a rep. He makes out. So naturally, I wanted to latch onto him. But he operates solo."

"How'd you find that out?"

"By circulating, how you think? You drop a query here and a query there, you know how it works. You see the way the guy dresses, whether he's got tailor-mades or the reg blues, whether he makes the most of his uniform in a good sailor town, or whether he wears civvies, things like that. I got to admit Daniels threw me at first. That crew cut, you know? I figured him for a boot. But he's a smart cookie. That haircut gives him a nice boyish look, makes the broads want to clutch him to their bosoms, you'll pardon me. He arouses—what would you call it—sympathy, I guess."

"And he's not married? You're sure of that?"

"If he is, sir, he's sure kept it a big secret."

"Yes, he certainly has."

"Now, maybe you're confusing his liberty maneuvers with marriage, sir."

"How do you mean, Caldroni?"

"Well, like I told you, this Daniels is good. He's nothing like Singer, you understand, because Singer never misses, never, sir, and that's the God's truth. But Daniels ain't bad so maybe you're confusing . . . Well, sir, it's almost *like* being married, when you get right down to it, I guess."

"What is, Caldroni?"

"You keep this under your hat, sir?"

"Certainly."

"Daniels, he don't confine his activities to the Norfolk theatre of operations, sir."

"He doesn't?"

"No, sir."

"Newport News?"

"Oh, without saying, sir. But Daniels got more far-reaching operations in hand, sir."

"How far-reaching?"

"Pretty far-reaching, sir. Leastwise, that's what Schaefer, Lord rest his soul, told me."

Masters sat rigidly at attention now. "Schaefer told you something about Perry Daniels?"

"Oh, yes, sir. 'Course, Schaefer turned out to be a killer and all, so maybe his word ain't so good, Lord rest his soul. But he told me this long before he bumped off that nurse, so maybe it's the truth. In fact, sir, I know part of it's the truth, 'cause I done some checking on my own." Caldroni paused. "Like I said, this is when I first came aboard, when I was still casting around for a prowlmate. Now, I got Singer, so I—"

"Never mind Singer, damnit! What'd Schaefer tell you? What'd you find out about Daniels?"

Caldroni's eyes opened wide. "Well, sir, I got to talkin' to Schaefer coupla times when I first come aboard. It don't hurt to know somebody in the Ship's Office. Never know when you're going to need a new I.D. card or a liberty—"

"What'd Schaefer tell you?"

"He was the one first tipped me off Daniels was a big man with the broads."

"What'd he say?"

"Said Daniels had a big network of steady shack-ups all over the country. Now, I don't know about all over the country, but I know Daniels was operating outside Norfolk. I checked."

"How?"

"Well, I figured this Daniels was a man to know, you know? So I begun watching the way he operated. Not in Norfolk, that boy. Oh, no. I followed him all the way to the train station once, just trying to find out where this boy had his deal. Asked the ticket guy after Daniels bought his ticket, Mr. Masters."

"Where did he go?"

"Shrewd cookie, this boy. This was when I was interested in becoming partners, so to speak. When I found out he was a lone wolf, well, hell, there wasn't no sense studyin' his operation no more. That's about when I run across Singer, right in the radar gang, right in my own backyard.''

"Where was Daniels going? The time you followed him to the railroad station?''

"Oh. Wilmington, sir.''

"Wilmington,'' Masters repeated.

"Yeah, he's got a nice little shack-up there, I'll bet,'' Caldroni said.

"Had,'' Masters said, and Caldroni eyed him quizzically.

A tall radarman with his white cap tilted back on his head sauntered down the aisle and sat in the seat next to the redhead.

"My name's Fred Singer,'' he said, smiling. "What's yours?''

12

It was early morning at N.O.B., Norfolk, Virginia. The mist that had clung to the front lawns of the base, spreading down from the barracks to the wide, winding concrete streets, had risen slowly, like a specter being called back to the grave at dawn, leaving the brick and the concrete drenched with a wintry sunlight. The men on the base lined up for chow, or made their sacks, or brushed their teeth. The four-to-eight watch was relieved, and on the ships tied up alongside the docks or moored in the bay the men lined up for muster.

In the hospital, a pharmacist's mate named Greg Barter brought breakfast to the man in 107. He wheeled the food in on a cart, and he put the glass of orange juice, the steaming bowl of cereal, the soft-boiled eggs, the slices of toast, the glass of milk onto the tray methodically and then shifted the tray to his patient's lap.

"Good morning, sir," he said cheerily, imitating the manner and friendliness of a hotel bellhop. "Is everything all right this morning, sir?"

"Everything's fine, thank you."

"Fever coming along nicely?" Greg asked.

"Very nicely, thank you."

"Does that mean it's going down, or steady as she goes?"

He looked at Greg warily. There was something about this bastard, something that needed watching. It was just his luck to have a character like this one rung in on him. Greg's eyebrows were raised in mild anticipation now, his face smug and wisely apprehensive.

"Steady as she goes, sir?" Greg asked.

"I think it's going down some," he answered.

"Ah, good, good. Nothing I like better than to see a man getting well. That's our job, you know. That's what all we poor hospital lackeys get paid for, isn't it? We're essentially pan handlers, but we like to see our dear little patients get on their feet again. Humanitarians, we are."

"I'll bet," he said.

"Ah, but we are," Greg answered. "Say, mate, would you like to hear an occupational joke? Sort of brighten up your morning, eh, speed you on the way to recovery?"

"If you like." He drank the orange juice and looked over at Greg.

"Where'd you go through boots?" Greg asked.

"What's it to you?"

"You don't like answering questions, do you?"

"No, I don't."

"Well, no matter," Greg said. "I went to Great Lakes. You familiar with Section Eight?"

"Yes."

"The nut-house unit, you know? Where they keep the psychos. Well, this story takes place in Section Eight. You listening?"

"I'm listening." He put some salt on his eggs and picked up a spoon.

"Want to eat that cereal, mate," Greg said kindly. "Give you your strength back."

"My eggs'll get cold."

"Sure, but eat your cereal, anyway."

He shrugged and picked up a tablespoon instead, digging into the cereal.

"Good, ain't it?" Greg asked.

"Yes."

"Well, this story. It's really a sort of riddle. You ready?"

"I'm ready.

"This pharmacist's mate," Greg said, "is making the

rounds in Section Eight, carrying the pan around, you see.''

"Yeah?"

"So, what did the pharmacist's mate say to one of the psychos?"

"I don't know. What *did* the pharmacist's mate say to one of the psychos?"

"Wanna peanut?"

"Huh?"

"Wanna peanut? Don't you get it? He's carrying around the pan, you see, and—''

"I get it,'' he said.

Greg shrugged. "Where's your sense of humor?"

"Listen, don't you have any other stops to make?"

"You're my last stop, Lover. Ain't you glad?"

"I'm tickled."

"You ever get a breakfast like that on your ship?"

"Sure,'' he said.

"Nah, not like this one. There's nothing like hospital duty, is there, mate?"

"My ship's a good one,'' he said.

"Which ship is that?'' Greg asked.

He hesitated. "The *Sykes*,'' he said at last.

"The *Sykes*. What's that, a DE?"

"A DD."

"Oh, a D . . . The *Sykes*, did you say?'' Greg's eyes narrowed. "You off the *Sykes*, huh?"

"Yeah. What's the matter with that?"

"Nothing." Greg paused, thinking. "You boys had a lot of trouble there recently, didn't you?"

"No trouble at all,'' he answered.

"I'm talking about Miss Cole,'' Greg said, his eyes squinched up tightly now.

"Oh, yeah. That.'' He shoved his cereal bowl aside and started on his eggs.

"FBI and everything, huh?"

"Yeah."

"What was this guy's name who did it?"

"Schaefer," he answered, his eyes on the egg.

"Schaefer. Sounds familiar. He ever pull duty here?"

"I wouldn't know."

"Yeoman, wasn't he?"

"Yeah."

"Mmmm."

"What's wrong with being a yeoman? Listen, ain't you got anyplace else to go? What's this? The local hangout?"

"I think I remember Schaefer. Yeah, I think so," Greg said. "He was here about when you were, wasn't he?"

"Who said I was here?"

"I said. I checked your records."

"What for?"

"I like to know my patients."

"Since when did you become a medic?"

"What are you getting riled about, mate?" Greg asked, his eyes studious and alert now.

"Who's getting riled? I just like to eat my breakfast without having to listen to a lot of crap."

"Did you know Miss Cole?"

"No," he snapped.

"Nice girl. You'da liked her, mate. The hot-pantsed type, but a nice girl."

"Too bad I didn't know her," he said warily.

"Yeah, too bad," Greg answered. "And you'll never get to know her *now*, will you? I mean, Schaefer killing her like that. Too bad."

"You gonna read a mass, or what?"

"What's the matter, mate?" Greg asked sweetly. "Don't you like me?"

"Not particularly," he answered. "Why the hell don't you shove off?"

"Sure," Greg said, and then his voice turned hard. "You'd better start looking sick again, pal. The doc'll be around any minute."

He turned his back and walked out of the room.

* * *

She came into 107 like a burst of sunlight. He had been waiting for her all afternoon, and now that she was here, he was truly excited. She was a damn good-looking girl, with good legs, better maybe than Claire's, and a nice innocent face that made you want to laugh and cry at the same time. She looked vulnerable, vulnerable as hell, and she was swallowing his line, he could see that. She didn't wear much lipstick, and her lips were ripe and perfectly formed, and he wanted to kiss those lips until they were bruised and red.

"Hi," she said from the doorway. "How's the sick man today?"

"Better, now that you're here."

"You're a fresh one," she said.

"Can I help it? A man comes in with plain old cat fever, and you cure that, but you give him a worse disease."

"Really? And what malicious ailment have you contracted here?"

"Heart disease," he said, his eyes serious.

"That's quite normal," Jean said lightly. "Every man falls in love with his nurse."

"And his nurse?"

"His nurse is here to take his temperature right now."

She shook down the thermometer, and he said, "The other side of the bed, Jean."

"Why?" she asked, puzzled.

"I like it better that way. I'm superstitious."

Jean shrugged. "All right," she said, sighing. "If you say so."

She walked around to the other side of the bed, so that the window was behind her, so that the sunlight streamed through the crisply starched uniform and the sheer slip beneath it, outlining her legs. He watched her legs, pleased with the way he had maneuvered her so that she was in silhouette, pleased with her vulnerability and her naïve innocence, thinking this one was going to be like falling off Pier Eight.

"Open," she said.

"You're pretty, Jean."

"Now stop that."

"You're lovely."

"Stop, I said."

"You're gorgeous."

"You're too talkative. Here." She rammed the thermometer into his mouth.

"Y've n'right abbe s'pretty," he said around the thermometer.

"Don't talk with the thermometer in your mouth," she warned, looking at her watch.

He took the thermometer out of his mouth for a moment. "You've no right to be so pretty," he repeated.

"Oh, now hush. And put that back in your mouth."

"Yes, ma'am," he said, saluting.

Jean giggled and turned away from him, walking to the window. He watched the lithe slender lines of her body. He could see the harsh elastic of her brassiere where it bit into the flesh of her back beneath the whitely transparent top of her uniform. This is better than a match, he thought. This is a damn fine way to raise a temperature. I wonder what she looks like in civvies. I wonder what she looks like in her underwear. Christ, she must look beautiful!

She turned from the window, the smile still on her face. "All right," she said, "Let's see how you're doing." She took the thermometer from his mouth and studied it. "Mmmm," she said.

"Am I dying?"

"No."

"Why don't people ever tell you your temperature? Doctors and nurses always make such a big mystery out of a thermometer reading."

"You're normal," she said.

"That's good," he answered. He paused. "But maybe it isn't, either."

"Why not? I should think you'd want to get out of here."

"I do, but . . ." He shook his head.

"What's the matter?"

"Jean, when I leave . . . I won't see you again, will I?"

"You're impossible, do you know that?"

"I'm serious now, Jean. I'd like to stay here forever. I'd like to be here with you forever."

She tried to laugh it off. "Well, I'm afraid that's a little impractical."

"I can think of something that isn't," he said rapidly.

"*Can* you? Well, well."

"Or . . . or don't you want to?"

"I want to take your pulse now, if that's what you're talking about," she said professionally. She took his wrist and looked at her watch.

"My heart's going like sixty," he said.

"It's not too bad."

"Jean, could you—do you think it's possible?"

"Do I think what's possible?"

"Seeing me? After I'm released from the hospital?"

She didn't answer him.

"Jean?"

"Shhh. I'm counting!"

"The hell with that," he said, pulling his wrist away and then catching her hand with his. "Answer me, Jean!"

He was holding her hand very tightly, and there was something electric about his grip. She thought of Chuck fleetingly, and the old debate rose in her mind again. *Was* she flinging herself at Chuck's head? Surely he was in New Jersey by now! Why hadn't he called? Or written?

"I . . . I think you'd better let me go," she said softly.

"No! Will you see me when I'm released, Jean?"

"I . . . I don't know."

"When *will* you know?"

"Please, someone may walk in."

"The hell with everybody, Jean! The hell with everybody but us! Just the two of us, honey, that's all, that's all that counts."

"Please let me go."

"Not until you answer."

"What do you want me to say?"

"That you'll go out with me."

"I have to think. Please . . ."

"Or is it the bar?" he asked.

There was no bitterness in his voice. There was, instead, an overwhelming sadness that instantly aroused her sympathy and her rage at the same time.

"Don't be ridiculous!" she snapped.

"It's against Navy Regs, you know."

"I know that. That has nothing to do with it."

"No?"

"No, nothing whatever."

He was close to home now. He sensed it instinctively, the way a fighter will sense the moment for the kill.

"You could get into trouble." He paused. "If we're not careful. Aren't you afraid of trouble?"

"Nursing—" She paused. "Nursing means a great deal to me."

He saw that she meant it, and he was frightened for a moment, afraid he had taken the wrong tack, afraid the whole thing would blow up in his face now.

"Of course," he said slowly, carefully, "no one would ever have to know, would they?"

"I . . . I suppose not."

He put her hand to his mouth suddenly, kissing the palm, kissing her wrist. His lips were moist and feverish. She tried to pull her hand away, but he held it tightly, pressing it to his cheek now.

"Say you'll come with me, Jean. Please, please. Can't you see how I feel about you? Doesn't it show? Jesus, can't you see I'd go nuts if I didn't see you again?"

"No no, don't say that. Please, you mustn't. You don't know. We . . . we've hardly met. We just . . ."

"Jean?"

"What? Oh, please let my hand go, won't you?"

"You'll go out with me?"

"Maybe. I don't know. Please, I have to think it out."

"You're beautiful," he whispered, and then he dropped her hand suddenly, and the hand felt curiously cold now that he'd released it. She brought the hand to her throat, avoiding his eyes. She could not deny that he had aroused something within her. She was confused and embarrassed by her own thoughts, and so she avoided his eyes and started for the door.

"Come back," he whispered. "Come back to me."

She hesitated and then looked back into the room. He was sitting up in bed, a sad smile on his face, looking pathetically weak. She wanted to hold him in her arms for a moment, wanted to comfort him, but she didn't know, she didn't know. She bit her lip.

"I will," she said. "I will be back."

"Understand you're about ready to get out of bed," Greg said.

"So they tell me," he answered.

"Well, good. I guess you're pretty damned anxious to get back to the *Sykes*. Must be an exciting ship, a destroyer."

"Stop snowing me, Greg. There isn't an exciting ship in the whole damn fleet."

"No?" Greg said, eyeing him carefully. He didn't like the way this was going. He could always get a rise out of 107, and today he wasn't doing so hot. The bastard looked too complacent today. That annoyed Greg. He liked needling this sonofabitch, he enjoyed it immensely. "Why, the *Sykes* seems to be a *real* exciting vessel, from where I sit. It ain't every ship in the fleet that gets a dead nurse." Greg watched. The bastard's eyes had flickered just a little bit. He didn't like talking about the ship or the nurse, especially the nurse. Well, if he didn't like it, that was just what Greg wanted.

Deftly, expertly, outraged by the idea of this malingering sonofabitch in 107, Greg applied the needle.

"They found her in the radar shack, huh?"

"Yes."

"You see her there?"

"No. How the hell would I get to see her?"

"I thought maybe you did."

"Say, what the hell's the matter? Were you in love with that broad or something?"

"Me?" Greg asked. "Hell, no. I'm just inquisitive."

"Well, go ask questions someplace else, will you? I'm gonna report you to the doc, you don't watch out."

"Oh, can it, pal!" Greg snapped. "You ain't reporting nobody to nobody."

"No, huh?"

"No! Don't you like talking about that dead nurse?"

"No, I don't. I don't like talking about anybody who's dead."

"That's 'cause you're a sickly type yourself."

"Yeah, that's right. I'm a sickly type,. And I'm sick of your crap, too, if you want to know something!"

"Now, what the hell are you getting excited about? Just because I happen to mention Miss Cole, and just because you had a sweet tooth for her last time you were—"

"Shut up! I didn't have a sweet tooth for nobody!"

That one had really got a rise, all right. He had damn near jumped out of the bed at that one. Greg's eyes narrowed. Carefully he pressed his advantage.

"You got to admit she was a nice-looking doll," he said sweetly.

"I never even saw her."

"But you were on her ward, pal. Don't you remember?"

"I don't remember anything about Claire Cole."

"Oh, you know her first name?"

"Of course I know her first name! What the hell's so unusual about that? Everybody on the *Sykes* knows her name. Damnit, she was killed on our ship!"

"Sure, I know that."

"O.K. O.K., if you know it, knock off. you're giving me a headache."

"Aw, now ain't that too bad? I didn't think talking about

Miss Cole would give you a headache. Aw, now I'm real
sorry, mate.''

"It's not talking about her that's giving me a headache.
It's just talking.''

"She was a nice girl. Shame that Schaefer bastard killed
her, ain't it?''

"Yes.''

"You think he was getting some of that?''

"I don't know.''

"It ain't impossible, you know. She was a hot number,
Miss Cole. The way I get it, she was spreading it around
everywhere. She was—''

"What do I care what Claire was—'' He stopped short.
The room was suddenly silent. Greg watched and
waited.

"—what Claire Cole was doing in her spare time? It's
none of my business.''

"No,'' Greg said, "of course not.''

"So lay off.''

"Sure. I just hate to see anybody knocking off the goose
that laid, you follow? Hell, she might have enlarged her
sphere of operations. Might have let some of us poor slobs
in on it, hey, chum? Wouldn't you have liked a little of
that, chum?''

"I don't even know what she looked like!''

"A nice-looking piece like Miss Cole? How could you
have missed her?''

"I don't know what she looked like,'' he insisted.

"Mmm,'' Greg said, "then you sure missed something.
She was a looker, mate, something to write home to
Mother about.''

"So why the hell don't you write home?''

Greg watched. Something was happening. The bastard
was beginning to clam up. Something had clammed him
up, and Greg was sure he wouldn't get another rise out of
him, not today he wouldn't. He tried anyway.

"Schaefer ever tell you what she was like?''

"No.''

"No kiss-and-tell stuff, huh?"

"I never asked."

"I'd think you'd be interested."

"Schaefer's business was Schaefer's business."

"Sure. Even though you were sweet on her, huh?"

"*You* said it, pal, not me."

"Yeah, but we both know it's the truth, don't we?"

"I only know what I read in the base newspaper."

"Did you read about how they found her? The bruises on her throat, skirt hiked all the way up? Did you read that, mate?"

"Yes, I read it."

"Must have been interesting."

"Very."

Greg rose. "I'll be seeing you, mate." He paused at the door. "A damn shame Schaefer knocked off your sweetie, ain't it?"

"Blow it out your ass," he replied, and then he rolled over and pulled the blanket to his neck.

She had avoided his room because she was unsure of her own feelings, and she wanted time to think. There was something very charming about him, something very young and appealing, even though she knew he was undoubtedly older than she was. But there was this—this almost pristine frankness of youth about him, and she enjoyed his frankness, and she also enjoyed his . . . well, yes, his adoration.

He was very different from Chuck, different in a sure, brash way, but at the same time the brashness wasn't annoying. Somehow, it wasn't annoying because she felt he wasn't being fresh just for the sake of being a wise guy; he was being fresh because he spoke his mind, and you could hardly classify that as freshness at all.

He was, too, a little frightening. Oh, not really frightening, but very masculine, she supposed that's what it was, yes, masculine. You could almost smell maleness on him, you could see it in his eyes, see it in the almost

cruel—and yet boyish—curve of his mouth. And this maleness frightened her, but it also aroused her until she had
difficulty remembering that Chuck was also a male, and
that Chuck had also aroused her. Why the devil didn't he
call or write or something?

This is all happening to me too late, that's the trouble,
she thought. I'm a novice at the game, and all because I
began playing it when most other girls were already expert
at it.

And there was, of course, the bar to think of. Not that
the title of ensign itself meant anything. No, that didn't
really matter a damn, did it? It was what the bar stood
for, the idea of nursing, the ideal of nursing, and she didn't
want all that to get washed out to sea simply because an
enlisted man was giving her a rush. And yet . . . they
could wear civvies, and who would know? And what harm
was there, actually, in seeing a movie together, or having
dinner together, both in civvies? How could anyone possibly know, and what harm was there? No harm, really,
unless you were caught.

But how could you get caught?

Oh, lots of ways. They could run into an officer she
knew, perhaps, an officer who knew her escort, too, and
who knew he was an enlisted man. But the chances of that
were remote, especially if they went to a movie, say, outside of Norfolk. They could even get up to Richmond and
back, for a movie, or dinner, or whatever, and really
there'd be no trouble at all, not if they were careful, and
they'd certainly have to be careful.

You simply had to figure whether or not it was worth it. If
Chuck would only write or let me know he's still alive . . .
Well, he probably doesn't care one way or the other. The
good Lieutenant's simply having himself a gay old time,
and yet he seemed sincere, and oh, Chuck, why don't you
hurry up back, can't you see I'm trying to decide something, and how can I really decide when you're somewhere
in New Jersey, and *he's* here, right here, with those eyes

of his and that cruel mouth, and those strong hands? Chuck, Chuck, can't you call? Don't you want to call me? She stayed away from Room 107 because she didn't want the decision forced upon her. And so she was surprised, and so she felt trapped, when she ran into him in the hospital corridor one night, wearing the faded robe and slippers of the ambulatory patient. She ran into him rounding a corner, and he caught her in his arms, and then backed her around the corner again, into a little dead-end passageway at the end of which was a gear locker and nothing else.

"Where've you been?" he whispered.

"Around the hospital. My . . . my hours have changed."

"Don't lie to me, Jean. If you don't want to have anything to do with me, say so. But please don't lie to me."

"I'm sorry. I was trying to make up my mind. That's why I—I've been avoiding you."

"Have you made it up yet?"

"No."

"When, Jean? I'll be out of here in a few days. You know that, don't you?"

"Yes, I know."

"Honey . . ."

"Please, don't rush me. Let me think. Can't you see that I . . ."

His hands were on her shoulders now, biting into the fabric of her uniform.

"Jesus, you're beautiful," he whispered. "Jean, Jean . . ."

He pulled her close, and she tilted her face involuntarily, and his lips came down on hers, strangely tender for such a cruel mouth. He was gentle and she was swallowed up in the tenderness of his kiss. She moved closer to him, and his arms tightened around her, and she returned the kiss, enjoying the tight circle of his arms, enjoying the strange gentleness of his mouth. She broke the kiss then, and his lips trailed over her jaw. She buried her head in his shoulder, still clinging to him, feeling a little weak now, a little dizzy from his kiss, and the tightness of his arms, the closeness of his body.

"You will, Jean?"

"Yes," she said. "I will."

"You want to?"

"I want to." She was still weak. She clung to him desperately, urging her senses to return.

"Friday," he said. "I'll be out by then. We'll go to a movie in Newport News. All right?"

"Yes." She pulled away from him. "You must let me go now. Someone might come."

"Eight o'clock, Jean," he said. "In civvies. You know the movie house there, don't you?"

"Yes."

"Eight o'clock Friday night. Jean, I—"

"Don't. Don't say it."

"All right. Later."

"Yes, later. Now please go."

He kissed her again, briefly, and then he whirled and went off down the corridor. She watched him until he was out of sight, and then she leaned against the wall limply and thought, Friday night, Friday night.

On Thursday afternoon they sat together in the sixth-floor solarium. The glass was in place now, against the onslaught of winter, glass that stretched from floor to ceiling, substituting for the screens that were up in summer. They sat together, the three men, and they looked through the glass and out over the base.

Guibert was the first to rise.

"I'm going down to take a nap. O.K., Greg?"

Greg nodded, saying nothing.

"One thing about a rare disease," Guibert said, "everybody treats you like a walking test tube. Hell, the whole future of mankind may depend on what they find out about me."

"You're priceless," Greg said. "Go on downstairs and

ask one of the nurses to lock you up in the vault. We wouldn't want to lose you."

"Greg's a card, all right," Guibert said. "Well, I'm going down." He paused. "Tennis, anyone?"

No one answered. Guibert shrugged and walked away.

He watched Guibert walk past Greg and then out into the corridor. In a little while, he heard the whine of the elevator, and then the doors rasping open and slamming shut, and then the whine again. He turned to Greg.

"You must be happy," he said.

"Yeah? Why?" Greg answered.

"I'm leaving tomorrow."

"We're gonna miss you, pal. It ain't often we get a professional goof-off like you around here."

He smiled. He could afford the luxury of a smile now. Now even Greg couldn't get under his skin. Everything was all set with Jean now. Tomorrow night, after that— hell, it would be simple.

"What're you grinning about?" Greg asked.

"Oh, nothing."

"I didn't think you'd be so happy about leaving. I notice you been real palsy-walsy with Miss Dvorak." Greg paused. "You ain't stepped out of line with her, have you?"

"Me?" he asked, feigning incredulity. "Hell, Greg, I know my place. Miss Dvorak's an officer."

"So was Claire Cole," Greg snapped.

"Well, I didn't know Claire Cole. But even if I did, I'd have respected those j.g. stripes."

"You knew her well enough to figure that, huh?"

"What?"

"That she was a j.g.?"

"Everybody on the *Sykes* knew that."

"Sure. Including Schaefer."

"Including Schaefer."

"He seemed like a nice kid, Schaefer. Not the kind you figure to be messing around with a broad. Not the kind who kills."

"No?"

"No." Greg paused. *"You* look more like the kind who kills to me."

"What do you mean by that?" He was sitting upright in his chair now, staring across at Greg. Greg's eyes had narrowed, and he looked into those eyes and realized he had responded too nervously. He would have to be careful.

"Yeah," Greg said slowly, as if an idea were forming in his mind. "Yeah, you look just like the kind who would kill."

"What the hell do you know about killers?" he asked calmly, watching Greg very carefully now, not liking the crafty look on the pharmacist's mate's face.

"Nothing. Only what I can smell. You smell like a killer to me. Yeah, you know that? You smell like a killer. You must be a real bastard in a fist fight."

"I can handle myself."

"Yeah, and better with women, I suppose."

"What are you talking about?"

"Must be easy to slam a dame around, huh?"

"I never hit a woman in my life."

"No?"

"No."

"Who hit Claire Cole?"

"Schaefer did."

"Yeah? Is that what it said in the base newspaper?"

"Yes, that's what it said."

"But we know different, huh?"

He was alert now, every sense alert. He stared at Greg and wondered if the pharmacist's mate were bluffing, how could he know, how could he possibly . . .

"What do you mean?" he asked.

"Claire and me used to talk together a lot," Greg said, the crafty look gleaming brightly in his eyes now.

"Yeah? Wh . . . what about?"

"Lots of things. Life. Liberty." Greg paused. "Men."

"What would she want to talk to you for, you crud?"

"I'm sympathetic. She told me all about Schaefer."

"Yeah?" He felt relieved. Greg knew nothing.

"And *you!*" Greg said suddenly.

"Me?" He snorted. "Hah, that's a laugh."

"How you were crazy about her," Greg said, his eyes narrowed, standing now, moving closer to the chair, his back to the huge glass area around the solarium.

"You're nuts."

"Real crazy about her. How you and her had a real ball here at the hospital, right under Schaefer's nose."

"Get out of here, will you? You're dreaming. You never talked to her."

"I did. Oh, yes, mate, I did."

Was Greg telling the truth? He couldn't be sure. Jesus, had Claire talked to him? But what was all this garbage about Schaefer? No, no, he was bluffing.

"You're bluffing me," he said.

"Bluffing about what?" Greg snapped.

"About . . . about talking to Claire. You never talked to her."

"Why should I bluff you? What's there to bluff you about? Why should I want to bluff you into anything?"

"You want me to say I knew Claire. You're needling me again, that's all." He glanced hastily around the solarium. They were alone, and he was thankful for that. No one else was listening to this conversation, no one but the two of them, alone up here.

"You got something to hide?" Greg shouted. "You think I don't know you knew Claire?"

"I *didn't* know her!"

"You're lying! You knew her here, and you knew her ashore, too!"

"What the hell! You're—you're—I didn't know her!"

"She said you did! She told me so. She said you were real chummy."

"She was lying, then. I didn't know her."

"She said you went to bed together!"

The accusation hung on the silence of the solarium. He sat watching Greg, aware of a thin sheen of sweat on his brow, now, wanting to know how much else Greg knew, wanting to know if this were true, uncertain now, thinking maybe, maybe . . .

"When did she tell you this?"

"Just before she died," Greg snapped, his eyes blazing. "Just before she went to the *Sykes.*"

"She . . . about me? She mentioned me?"

Greg moved forward swiftly, his lips skinned back over his teeth, his eyes bright. "She said she was going to the *Sykes* to meet you! That's what she said!"

He leaped out of his chair. "You tell this to anyone?"

Greg backed off a pace, his face suddenly pale. "You . . . you . . ." He was fighting for ideas now, and fighting for breath. "Why, you . . . This is all true, ain't it?" Greg's eyes were wide in astonishment now, and something else. Fear. He was backing away quickly, as if he expected an attack. "I—I was just making it up, trying to get a ri . . . But it's true! Holy Jesus, you killed her, didn't you? Holy Jesus, you killed Claire Cole!"

He shoved out at Greg, and Greg stumbled backward a pace, and then he shoved again, harder this time, and Greg floundered for balance, losing his footing, going back, back. He closed in on Greg, and this time he shoved with all the weight of his shoulder and arms behind the push. He saw Greg lunge backward, and then he heard the crash as Greg's body hit the glass. The body clung there for a moment, and then the glass shattered and the body rushed out to meet the cold winter air, eyes wide, hands clawing at nothing.

He rushed out of the solarium, hearing footsteps down the corridor, ducking around a corner where he was unseen.

When Greg hit the pavement, six stories below, his eyes were still wide in astonishment and disbelief, and his skull cracked open with an angry splash that blotted everything out of his mind and his body.

13

THE B-26 WAS PAINTED YELLOW, AND IT HUNG AGAINST
the gray sky like an egg yolk on a city pavement. Its nose
was pointed toward the New Jersey coastline, and its en-
gines droned monotonously. Up in the cabin, the pilot and
co-pilot damn near fell asleep.

On the island of Brigantine, off the New Jersey coast,
there stood a hotel. The hotel had once been headquarters
for Father Divine and his angels, but it had been taken
over by the Navy for a radar school, and its roof bristled
with antennae now. The Sugar Roger antenna, the large
bedspring type attached to the air-search gear, revolved
with methodical precision, circumscribing a 360-degree
impenetrable area of electronic impulses. The impulses
leaped through the air, reaching out and out, striking the
metal skin of the B-26, bouncing off that skin, echoing
back through the nonresisting atmosphere, were caught
again by the all-seeing eyeless bedspring antennae, chan-
neled down into the depths of the hotel via a thick cable,
translated onto the circular P.P.I. scope in terms of short
electronic visual spurts of brightness, and retranslated by
the radar operator in terms of range and bearing.

Fred Singer depressed the button on top of his sound-
powered phones. "Bogey," he said, "three-one-zero,
range thirty."

A radarman named Rook, wearing sound-powered
phones, one earpiece in place, the other shoved onto his
temple so that he could hear messages on the phones and
orders from Mr. Masters simultaneously, picked up a thick
black crayon and applied it to the plastic surface that

143

stretched in front of him. The plastic was etched with a large wheel, the hub of which was the hotel, the spokes of which were the relative bearings from 360 degrees, around to 090 degrees, to 180 degrees, to 270 degrees, back to 360 degrees. Circles within circles, marking off the ranges—ten miles, twenty miles, thirty miles, forty miles, and out, out, out—crossed the bearing markers. Automatically, Rook found 310, followed the range markers out to thirty miles, marked a large X on the plastic at the intersection. Writing backward, so that the writing was visible and intelligible for Mr. Masters, standing on the other side of the clear plastic, he jotted down the time in minutes and quarter minutes: 07[8].

Singer called in another reading a minute later. Rook marked another X and connected both X's with a straight line. Another reading, another X, another reading, another X. On the plastic, writing backward, Rook drew a box and inside the box he indicated: Course, 190. Speed, 250.

From the radar gear, Singer asked, "Request permission to stop Sugar Roger antenna."

Masters snapped down his button. "Permission granted," he said.

Singer snapped a dial, adjusted another. The operation couldn't have taken more than forty seconds. Into his phone he said, *"Single* bogey."

Rook automatically wrote this onto the plastic. They now knew they had an unidentified aircraft (which they'd known all along, since the B-26 was simulating an enemy plane and they had been informed of this before the practice session began) that was traveling at a speed of 250 miles an hour on a course of 190, which meant it would be on the hotel in a matter of minutes.

Masters pulled down a hand mike. "Blue One, this is Blue Base," he said. "Over."

Caldroni, who was playing the role of the squadron commander leading the interceptor planes known as Blue One, answered, "This is Blue One. Over."

"Single bogey," Masters said, glancing at the plastic again. "Three-one-zero, range twenty-two, course one-nine-zero, speed two-fifty." Rapidly he calculated an intercepting course. "Vector two-one-zero, angels five. Over."

"Wilco and out," Caldroni said.

On the plotting board before him Caldroni plotted his own squadron's progress, together with the progress of the oncoming B-26. The B-26 moved relentlessly toward its target, which was the hotel. Caldroni's squadron, for which they had calculated a top speed of 350 miles an hour, had a hell of a long way to go before visual contact could be made.

Masters picked up the hand mike again. "Blue One, this is Blue Base. Over."

"This is Blue One," Caldroni said. "Over."

"Tallyho?" Masters asked, wanting to know if, according to the plotting Caldroni was doing, the squadron had as yet sighted the enemy aircraft.

"Not yet, sir," Caldroni said. "Over."

"Out," Masters said sourly. The men all looked up as they heard the sound of the B-26 overhead. "We were just blown off the map," Masters informed them. "You all did one hell of a sloppy job." He picked up a live mike and said, "Yellow One, this is Charley Horse. Over."

Static erupted into the darkened room. Then the pilot of the B-26 answered, "Go ahead, Charley Horse."

"Want to take another run, please? Over."

"Roger. Give us a vector. Over."

"Vector three-one-zero, angels three. Choose your own approach. We want to be surprised. Start out at about a hundred and fifty, will you? We want to see what kind of range pickup we've got."

"Hope you've got plenty of time," the pilot said. "This buggy can't do much more'n two hundred and fifty per. This ain't a jet, you know."

"I know," Masters said. "We'll be ready for you when you come back."

"They should've put this crate in moth balls years ago," the pilot muttered, and then he added, "Out."

Masters turned to Singer. "What the hell's wrong with you, Singer? Were you asleep?"

"I was getting a lot of land-mass echo, sir."

"Baloney," Masters said. "There's nothing between you and England but the Atlantic ocean."

"Must be high waves, then, sir."

"Come on, Singer, get on the ball. You pick him up at thirty miles, and he's on us before we can get a plane to him. All right, let's leave this for now. I want all of you in Room Thirty-three in ten minutes. Take a smoke, and be there on the button. We're going to try a few torpedo runs."

"We did that already," Kraus, another of the radarmen, complained.

"And we'll keep doing it until we get it right," Masters snapped. "Go take your smokes."

Andrew Brague, an ensign fresh out of communications school, walked over to Masters. "Think we're riding them too hard, sir?"

"What?" Masters said, wondering why every idiot ensign in the world eventually came under his wing.

"The men, sir. Don't you think you're being a little hard on them?"

"How so?" Masters asked, annoyed.

"No liberty since we've been here. Round-the-clock watches. Classes every minute except for chow and smoke breaks. I don't know, sir."

Masters eyed Brague sourly. "Tell me, Ensign," he said, "just what the hell you think this is—a picnic?"

"Sir?" Brague said, startled.

"We're here to unify these men into a smoothly working machine. We're going to be a picket ship, Brague. Do you know what that means? It means that the life of the *Sykes* and the life of the task force behind the *Sykes* will depend upon the efficiency of our radar screen. Do you know what the average life span of a picket ship on station is, Brague?''

''No, sir.''

''It's measured in minutes, Brague,'' Masters said. ''I don't want to wind up as a statistic. So I'm trying to pound some working knowledge into the heads of these men. This may all be a joke to them now, but someday it may be serious, damned serious, and I think we should be ready, don't you?''

''Well of course, sir.''

''Then don't tell me I'm riding the men too hard. I'll ride them as hard as I have to, and there'll be no liberty until I can see something sinking in. Have I been ashore yet, Brague?''

''No, sir.''

''Damn right I haven't. And I'll tell you something else, Brague. There's a girl I've been dying to call for the past week. She's in Norfolk right now, and that's where I'd like to be, and I want her to know that. But every time I come within six yards of that phone booth in the lobby, there's always somebody coming along with another damn order from the C.O. of this joint. I haven't even had time to write her a letter! So don't come weeping to me about the men. We're all 'men,' Brague, and to hell with Navy jargon. And I don't like this any more than the rest of us.''

''Yes, sir.''

''Don't look so damn sad. Round up the rest of the officers, and we'll have a conference on this torpedo stuff before the run-through. Bring your cigarettes.''

''Yes, sir.''

''Brague?''

''Yes, sir?''

''Would you like to take my mid-watch tonight? So that I can finally get that letter off?''

Brague looked militantly disappointed. ''If you say so, sir.''

''Skip it. I was just kidding. Get your cigarettes and your fellow officers. We've got a lot of work to do.''

* * *

On the base at Norfolk there was talk, lots of talk.

"Sure, I knew Greg Barter," the talkers said. "Hell of a nice guy. But I understand he was an attendant in the booby hatch at Bethesda. That stuff's contagious, you know."

"Greg Barter, yes," the talkers said, "a good man, one of my best. Inclined toward melancholia, however. Should have forseen this, should have sensed it coming. Well, you never know when a suicidal tendency will emerge full blown, do you? Eh?"

"I spotted him for a nut from go," the talkers said.

The talkers said, "Greg thunk too much. When you start thinking, you find out you don't like yourself so much. Bang! You jump out the window."

And the talkers said, "I liked Greg. You can't tell me he jumped through that glass. He musta slipped."

"All alone in the solarium," the talkers said. "Who the hell knows *what* happened, really?"

"One guy knows," the talkers said, "and that's Greg Barter, and he ain't telling it to nobody but Saint Peter."

There were *two* men who knew.

One of them might or might not have been telling it to Saint Peter.

The second was telling it to nobody.

He stood in the head and shaved carefully, very carefully. He wanted to look good tonight. This was the first time she'd be seeing him in anything but pajamas or a robe, and he felt that the first impression was the most important one.

Jean Dvorak, Lamb Being Led to Slaughter.

Well, not exactly to slaughter. To Wilmington would be more like it. And not tonight, of course. Tonight was the preliminary bout, so to speak. The main event would come later, depending on what happened tonight. He had no doubts about how tonight would turn out. He was sure of her already. She was a confused kid, yes, but the confused kids were the best kind. She didn't know which end was up, and she wouldn't know until he showed her, and he was looking forward to the demonstration with considerable relish.

Confused, but gorgeous. With that nice pure beauty, that unspoiled kind of beauty, like a field of snow waiting for footprints. Oh, Jesus, how innocent!

Her innocence pained him. It was almost too excruciating to bear. Claire had been beautiful, but she was wise and knowing, and a little hard, he supposed, but beautiful, yes, beautiful, hell, you couldn't take that away from her. But you couldn't deny she was hard either. He'd spotted her instantly, spotted her as an easy mark—*if* he appealed to her. He knew she was the kind you had to appeal to. She was hard, but she wasn't petrified. And he'd appealed to her because he knew which approach to take. The right approach was the most important thing, of course. With Jean, you had to put things on an emotional plane, the undying-love pitch. Well, he was ready to give her his undying devotion, but there were strings, of course, and the strings weren't too painful, were they? Shouldn't love be unselfish? Of course, Jean. And isn't our love a beautiful, fragile, tender thing? Jean, can't we . . . Couldn't we . . .

Damn right we can, he thought, smiling.

From the sink opposite him, Petroff, a gunner's mate said, "You back already?"

"Yeah," he answered.

"What'd you have?"

"Cat fever."

"Yeah, I had that once," Petroff said. "Hey, was you there when that pecker checker took the plunge?"

"Was I *where?*" he asked.

"At the hospital, natch."

"Oh. Yes."

"Musta been a psycho, huh?"

"Definitely nuts," he answered.

"Boy, Norfolk's sure gettin' its share."

"Yeah."

"First the broad, then Schaefer, then this jerk. This town is jinxed."

"I'm trying to shave," he answered.

"O.K., O.K., shave." Petroff turned away angrily, obviously hurt by his shipmate's indifference.

He watched Petroff in the mirror for a moment, and then turned his attention from the gunner's mate, smiling. Jean Dvorak was still on his mind, a ripe fig waiting to be plucked and swallowed whole. One bite. *Zoom,* down the hatch. And after that . . . Hell, after the first time, it was easy.

Like murder.

He didn't like thinking about murder, but he had to admit it got a little easier each time. Especially when you got away with it. And getting away with it was almost as easy as the actual killing. Now there was a disgusting word. Well, that's what it was. A rose by any other name . . . Jesus, but Jean smells sweet. Not a perfume smell, no, just a good soap smell, clean, like everything about her. Oh, this is going to be a peach, this is going to be like nothing ever.

That sonofabitch Greg, of course, never knew what hit him. An object lesson for all practical jokers. Play with fire, and you wind up with your brains scattered on the concrete. I should have spotted his bluff right away, but Jesus, he sounded like he had the goods. Well, he's got the goods now, but a lot it's going to get him. Maybe a cloud and a harp. Or maybe a pitchfork and an asbestos suit. Serve the bastard right. He shouldn't have played with me that way. I can't take chances now. Murder has come easy, but it won't be so easy if I'm caught, and so I've got to be careful, very careful now. The slightest hint, and then I move again. I have to. I can't take chances. Claire was a snap, and so was Schaefer—but Schaefer knew, and so did Greg. Well, he knew for a second before he found himself doing a swan dive. Anybody who knows is a dan-

ger to me. Anybody who knows is leading me straight to
the gallows, helping me slit my own throat.

He rinsed his razor, and then he washed the lather from
his face. He ran the back of his hand along his cheek.
Smooth. Jean would like that. Jean didn't go for the gorilla
type. Jean wanted it tender and gentle, like an opening
bud. Well, Bud, I'm just the man to fill the bill. Shake
hands.

She was waiting in front of the movies at eight sharp.
She wore a sweater and skirt and because it was a brisk
night, a tweed topper. She wore seamless stockings and
dark-blue pumps. A long string of pearls trailed over the
rise of her bosom beneath the topper. She had tucked her
blonde hair under a kerchief, but a pale wisp had come
loose, and it hung limply on her forehead now.

She was slightly nervous, and she watched the faces of
the passersby, alternately looking for him and then for
someone who might be able to identify her. She was aware
of the pounding of her heart beneath the woolen sweater.
She was very ill at ease, and she felt sneaky, but she did
want to see him because she had to know exactly what she
felt, had to determine in her own mind just what was what.

When the car pulled to the curb, she figured it for a
pickup attempt. She glanced at it quickly, and then turned
her head away.

She turned to the car again. It was he, behind the wheel
of the car!

He opened the door for her, not getting out of the car,
and she walked to it hastily and climbed in, slamming the
door behind her.

"Hi," he said.

"Hi. Where'd you get the car?"

"I hired it. You don't really feel like going to a movie,
do you?"

"Well, I don't know. What did you have in mind?" She
hoped she hadn't sounded coy, because she honestly hadn't
intended to.

"A drive, I thought. Look at all those stars, Jean. Millions of them."

"Yes," she said. "They're lovely, aren't they?"

"And maybe a hamburger and some good hot coffee afterward. Are you game?"

"Whatever you say," she said, smiling.

He pulled the car away from the curb. It was a late-model convertible, but the top was leaky, and she felt chilly.

"You look pretty," he said.

"Thank you."

"How do I look?"

She glanced over at him. He was wearing a heavy tweed overcoat, and a blue suit, she supposed; it was very hard to tell in the dim interior of the car. She thought he looked very handsome, though, and she said, "You look nice."

"Disappointed?"

"No."

"Good. Where to?"

"Anywhere. You're driving."

"O.K., fine. You *didn't* feel like a movie, did you?"

"To tell you the truth, I'm still a little nervous," she said.

"Well, relax. That's one of the reasons I got the car. I figured you'd feel more secure."

"I do."

"Good."

"I guess it's just—Oh, things have been in an uproar at the hospital. I mean, it may be that. It may have something to do with this."

"What kind of an uproar?" he asked.

"Well, you saw the bedlam when you checked out this morning, didn't you?"

"Greg, you mean?"

"Yes. Wasn't that a terrible thing? He was such a nice boy."

"Yeah, he seemed like a nice guy."

"Sometimes I think—Oh, never mind."

"What?"

"Well, we were always very friendly, Greg and I. He was a nice person to work with, do you know what I mean? Always a cheerful word. We talked a lot, especially when we had the night duty together. He played the violin, did you know that?"

"No."

"Yes, he did. Not very well, I suppose, but he had a feeling for it. He was really a very gentle person under that rough exterior of his."

"Yes, he seemed to be a nice gentle guy."

"And I got to know him pretty well, which is why I feel . . . well, it's almost like the kiss of death. Everything I touch. Claire Cole and now Greg."

"Jean, that's a silly way to feel. You don't mind my saying so, do you?"

"I can't help it, it's just the way I feel."

"Well, it's just silly, really. Hell, Claire Cole was killed on my ship. Now, I don't feel any—"

"Are you off the *Sykes?*" she asked suddenly.

"Yes. Didn't you know?"

"No. No, I didn't."

"Well, sure. And she was killed right there, and so was this guy Schaefer. According to your logic, the whole crew should go around feeling guilty. Now, that's silly."

"Schaefer," she said softly. "The yeoman. Yes."

"You didn't know him, did you?"

"No. I just . . . knew *of* him."

"Oh, yeah. Nice guy."

"He . . . he committed suicide, too, didn't he?"

"Yes," he said.

"Funny."

"What's funny?"

"Two suicides. So close together."

"Yeah. Say, are you chilly in here? I can turn on the heater."

"No, no, I'm fine." She shook her head. "Poor Greg.

You were in the solarium with him just before he—he jumped, weren't you?''

"Who?"

"You. I thought—''

"What gave you that idea?''

"Guibert said so. He said he left you and Greg alone up there.''

"Oh. Oh, sure. Yeah, I went down a few minutes after Guibert. Nice kid, that Guibert, isn't he? It's a pity he's got that dis—''

"Did Greg say anything to you that might indicate he was—''

"Oh, nothing really. He was just looking sort of morose. In fact, that's why I left. He was too damn sad for me.''

"Yes.'' She was very quiet now, thinking.

"Mind if I stop the car?'' he asked.

"What?''

"The car. All right if I pull over?''

"Oh. Oh, yes, if you want to.'' She looked up at her surroundings. The road was very dark, and he was pulling off the road, into a little clearing in the woods. He cut off the motor and then leaned back against the seat. "Look at those stars, Jean.''

"Yes.'' She paused. "You never mentioned you were off the *Sykes* before.''

"No? Guess it never came up.''

"Did you know Schaefer well?''

"To talk to.'' He put his arm on the seat behind her.

"Do you know Lieutenant Masters?''

"Yes.'' He moved closer to her. "You know, you talk an awful lot for such a pretty girl.''

"Lieutenant Masters has a theory,'' she said, absorbed in her thoughts. "Lieutenant Masters thinks—'' She cut herself off suddenly turning her head slowly to look at him.

His arm tightened around her shoulder. "What does he think?'' he asked idly.

"Nothing," she said. Her mind was racing, suddenly alert. She tried to think clearly, tried to think of the names Chuck had mentioned. Yes, yes. That night on the bay . . .

"And you still think one of those two men did it? What were their names?"

"Daniels and Jones. Perry Daniels and Alfred Jones."

She was cold all at once. Why hadn't she made the connection before? How could she have been so stupid?"

"Jean?"

She sat bolt upright. "Yes?"

"Anything wrong?"

"No," she said. I may be sitting here with a murderer, she thought. He may have killed Claire and Schaefer. And Greg! Oh, God, Greg!

He pulled her to him, and his lips sought hers, and they left her strangely cold this time, but she returned his kiss, wondering how she could know for sure, how she could find out for sure. She was breathing rapidly now, her breasts rising and falling. He kissed her feverishly, mistaking the tempo of her breathing for something else.

"Jean," he whispered, "I love you."

She was silent. His kisses traveled over her neck, her ear, her cheeks, her closed eyes, the tip of her nose. His hands were tight on her shoulders. "I love you, I love you, I love you," he repeated endlessly, and she listened to the crooning of his voice, and she thought only that he could be a murderer, that he could have pushed Greg off the solarium. The thought frightened her, and she began to tremble, and again he mistook the harsh breathing and the trembling, and his hand dropped idly to the pearls around her neck, his fingers toying with them, close to her breasts, rising and falling.

"Aren't you going to say anything?" he asked, his fingers exploring each separate bead, fondling the pearls.

"What . . . what do you want me to say?"

"Something. I've just put my heart on my sleeve. Doesn't that call for a comment?"

"I . . . I don't know yet."

His hand dropped from the pearls casually, almost accidentally. She felt the warmth of his fingers on her, and her first reaction was to pull away, but she controlled her fear, and she asked, "Have you loved many girls?"

"None like you," he said.

"But many?"

His hand moved in a gently stroking motion, the fingers tightening, tightening. He pulled her closer to him, more sure of himself now, sure of the freedoms he could take with her body, sure of his charm. "I've never really loved anyone, Jean," he said. "This is really love."

"How do you know?" she asked, feeling the fingers caressing her, wanting him to stop, but not daring to stop him because she wanted to hear what he had to say, wanted to lead him to say what she wanted to hear.

"I just know. I want you terribly and so I know I love you. I've never felt like this before."

"It's biology," she said. "You don't really care about me. You just want—"

"No, no." His hand tightened on her involuntarily. "No, Jean, honestly. I want you because I love you."

"I think you're . . . you're in love with my uniform. The idea of—getting a nurse—an officer."

"No, I swear. That isn't it."

"It is. I can feel it. I know it is."

"Jean, believe me—"

She stopped his hand and moved to the other side of the car. "No," she said, feigning injury. "I know that's what it is. I'm an officer. You're just excited by the idea, that's all."

He scrabbled across the seat toward her. "Jean, that's not so. Jean . . ." He pulled her to him, kissing her, his hand lingering on her throat and then dropping again, fumbling with the buttons on the cardigan, grasping. "Jean, I'm nuts about you. I want you so bad I could—"

"Stop," she said. "Please stop! You're lying to me."

"What the hell do I care whether or not you're an offi-

cer?'' he shouted desperately, his hand touching thin silk
now. "You think that matters to me? You think I care
about that?''

"Yes. That's all you care about.''

"I've been out with officers before!'' he blurted.

She caught his hand at the wrist, holding it away from
her body. "Not a nurse!'' she said.

"Yes, a nurse. Yes, Jean, I've been out with a nurse.''

"Who?''

"Somebody. Jean . . .''

She released his hand and he caught at her body again.
"Who?'' she asked.

"A nurse. We were very close.''

"How close?''

"Very close. Jean, we could be close, too.''

"Yes,'' she said reflectively, wanting him to tell her
more.

"Monday,'' he said almost crooning the word, his confidence back now, his confidence strong and firm in the
fingers that candidly caressed her body. "Are you free
Monday?''

"Yes,'' she murmured.

"We could go somewhere. Just the two of us.''

"Where could we go?''

"I know places. We could be together, Jean.''

"Like you and this other nurse?'' she probed.

"Just you and me, Jean,'' he said, ignoring her question. "Just the two of us. We could be . . . very close,
darling, very close.''

"Where?''

"There's a place in Wilmington,'' he said.

"Wilmington,'' she repeated dully.

"Yes. We'd go in civvies. No questions asked. Jean,
you do want to, don't you?''

"I don't know,'' she said.

"I'll call you. I'll call you tomorrow. You'll know by
then, won't you?''

"I don't know." She stopped his hand again. "I think we'd better go now."

"I'll call you tomorrow," he said. "Tomorrow morning. You sleep on it, Jean. I'll call you."

"All right," she said.

"When I call I don't want to take any chances on anybody listening in. I'll say I'm . . . I'm Frank, O.K.? I'll say I'm Frank, and you'll know who it is."

"Yes."

He kissed her again, longingly, and his hands traveled to her waist and she sat up and squeezed her eyes shut tightly and moved away from him.

"Monday," he said. "Monday."

"I'll see," she answered.

14

THE ROOM WAS VERY WARM AND VERY STILL. THE SUN-
light streamed through the window, illuminating the dust
motes, sending them scattering like vagrant flecks of dan-
druff.

Is it Saturday morning already? Jean thought. Has the
night really passed?

She lay naked in bed, the sheet pulled to her throat, the
blanket wadded down at the foot of the bed. She soaked
in the sunshine, feeling its warmth on the sheet and her
body beneath the sheet, not wanting to stir, not wanting
to get out of bed, not wanting to face any decisions this
morning. It would be so nice just to lie there forever,
warm and secure, with the sun toasting her body, covering
her with a warm, secure . . .

Her body.

She stared down the length of the sheet, watching the
rise and fall of her breasts, the sharp nipples etched against
the thin fabric, the curves of her thighs, the flatness of her
stomach. It looked soft and vulnerable, a woman's body.
It did not look like a weapon.

She had never considered her body as a weapon before,
but she knew now that it was one, a very formidable
weapon. He would call this morning, and he would expect
a decision, expect to know about Wilmington on Monday.
Wilmington, of course, didn't matter at all. Anywhere
would have done just as well. Wilmington was just a town
he'd picked, a town he knew, the town Claire had gone
to. He'd told her he'd dated a nurse before—but was that
nurse Claire? Was he the one who'd killed her?

Perry Daniels and Alfred Jones, or so Chuck had said. Of course, Chuck might have been all wet to begin with, in which case there was nothing to worry about; in which case she certainly didn't want to go to Wilmington for a day. But supposing Chuck had been right, and supposing that man *were* the killer—then what? She could go to the *Sykes,* that's what she could do. She could speak to the Captain and say, "This man is a killer. I want you to put him in the brig."

Except that the case was closed, as far as the Captain was concerned. Chuck had made that point very emphatically. The case was closed as far as everyone but Chuck was concerned. Chuck and the real murderer. And now me. Now I'm in it.

And I *can* find out if this is the man or not, she thought. I can find out easily because my body is a weapon. It's comical how strong a weapon it's become, but with this man it definitely is a weapon, and I know he would tell me what I want to know—if I use my body as a weapon. But if he is a murderer, and if I find out what I want to know, what then? If he is a murderer, then he's killed three times already, and what will he do to me when he finds out I've tricked him, when he realizes he's given me his secret? And *will* he tell me, anyway? Suppose I do go along with him to Wilmington? What happens when we're alone? Suppose he tells me nothing? Suppose he refuses to talk, suppose he only wants . . .

Can I scream for help?

Did Claire Cole scream for help?

If he's a murderer, he's dangerous, and if I go with him, I'm taking a chance, a great risk. And why should I care, really?

He may be a murderer!

Yes, yes, but why does it have to be me? I don't want to go with him. I don't want to be alone with him again, not in Wilmington, not anywhere. Even if he isn't a killer, he frightens me. Oh, why can't Chuck be here? Chuck darling, why can't you be here?

"Jean?"

She turned her head toward the door abruptly, surprised by the voice. "Yes?"

"Telephone for you."

"Oh." She lay motionless, the dust motes floating around her.

"You going to answer it? I can tell him you're not around, if you like."

"No. No, I'll take the call." She waited until the other nurse was gone, and then she got out of bed and slipped on a robe and a pair of loafers, belting the robe tightly at her waist. She went to the phone outside in the corridor, biting her lips, wondering what she would say to him. Nervously she picked up the receiver.

"Hello?" she said in a small voice.

"Jean? Did I wake you?"

"No. I was . . . I was up."

"This is Frank."

"Yes," she said. "Yes, I know."

"Well?"

There was a long silence on the line.

"Are you coming with me?" he asked.

"I . . ." She hesitated, biting her lip again. Then she said, "All right, Frank. I'm coming with you."

"Good. Jean, I've got a fix in. I can get off the ship in time to catch the eight-fifteen bus on Monday morning. That's the C and O bus to the Hampton Roads transfer, where we can get a train to Wilmington. Do you know where the terminal is?"

"I'll find it," she said.

"Good. If we catch that bus, we can be in Wilmington at three-forty-two. And I don't have to be back until muster the next morning. O.K.?"

"Yes."

"Look, we won't even talk to each other until we're far away from Norfolk. O.K.? Don't even look at me when we get on the bus. And wear civvies, don't forget."

"I won't."

"I love you," he whispered.

She said nothing. She held the phone in a cold hand, waiting for his voice again.

"Jean?"

"Yes?"

"Monday morning, eight-fifteen, the C and O bus. Have you got that?"

"Yes, I've got it."

"You'll be there, won't you?"

"I'll be there."

"Fine. I've got to hurry back before they miss me." He paused. "Do you love me?"

She didn't answer. She hung up gently, hoping he would think she'd hung up during his pause. Then she sat down in the chair beside the phone, her temples throbbing.

She went down the dock that afternoon, as soon as she was off duty. The weather was turning really cold, and a damp gray sky hung over the water. Her coat was buttoned to the throat, and it whipped about her legs as she strode over the wood plankings. An oil tender was tied up at the dock, but it was the only ship in sight. And her heart lurched into her throat in apprehension. Had the *Sykes* left?

She stared out over the water, trying to distinguish the ships in the harbor. Maybe the *Sykes* was out for a short run.

When the voice sounded behind her, she wheeled in panic.

"Can I help you, miss?"

He was a young boy, the collar of his pea coat turned up high, the guard belt slung low on his waist. He carried a billy, and his face was raw and red from the wind that blew in over the water.

"I . . . I'm looking for a ship. The *Sykes*. A destroyer," she said.

The boy smiled. "Oh, yeah. She went into dry dock, miss. You can find her there. You know the ship, miss?"

"Yes, I do."

He gave her directions, and she nodded, and then he saluted her before she left. She felt awkward returning his salute, the way she always felt whenever a man acknowledged her rank. She tried to tell herself it was the same thing as someone tipping his hat to you, but she knew that wasn't true, and it always left her feeling a little embarrassed. She walked up the dock, her heels clicking on the plankings, terribly aware of her body today, aware of it as she had never been in all her life before. She knew the boy's eyes were on her back and her legs, and she consciously stiffened, trying to avoid the unconscious feminine swing of her hips. She was glad when she was off the dock, and she told herself she'd imagined the low whistle she'd heard, that it was simply the wind blowing off the water.

There was a great deal of activity in the dry-dock area; trucks and jeeps scurrying over the ground, cables and torches and welding masks. The rusted hulls of ships rested on their metal beds, and the workmen tore out their guts. She picked her way carefully over the ground, avoiding the large spools of cables, the heavy sheets of metal. She spotted the *Sykes,* high above her, and she saw the narrow wooden planks leading to the ship's main deck.

Good heavens, she thought, I'll never get up there.

She was conscious of the eyes of the workmen, conscious too of the fact that *his* eyes, unseen, might be watching her from somewhere aboard the ship, and she wished she'd never come here. She looked up at the ship again, saw the OD stepping aside to let a workman with a cylinder of oxygen past. She waved abruptly, knowing it was a very unmilitary thing to do, but doing it anyway.

The OD strolled to the rail and shouted over the clamor of the workmen. "Yes, miss?"

"I wonder if you could tell me—"

The OD cocked his head and shouted, "I'm sorry, miss. I can't hear you. Just a moment."

She watched as he left the quarter-deck and navigated

across the wooden plank. He climbed down to where she was standing, and she saluted when he approached, and he returned the salute casually.

"Now then," he said, "what can I do for you?"

She turned her back toward the ship. "I'm trying to locate Lieutenant Masters," she said.

A smile began forming on the OD's face, and she wondered, God, is that all every man thinks of?

"Well," the OD drawled slowly, "I'm awfully sorry, miss, but Masters isn't aboard. In fact, there's hardly *anyone* aboard."

"Yes, I know. But I was wondering . . . do you know where I can reach him?"

"In Atlantic City." The smile was broader now.

"*Where* in Atlantic City?" Jean asked.

"Well, not exactly Atlantic City," the OD said. "He's at radar school, miss. Brigantine, New Jersey."

"Brigantine," she repeated thoughtfully.

"Maybe . . . ah . . . *I* can help miss?"

"I don't think so," Jean said. "Do you know when he'll be back?"

"Yes, miss. In a week or so."

"I see." He kept smiling at her, and she felt warm and hoped she wasn't blushing. "If I were to write a letter—I mean, do you know the address?"

"If you just address it U.S.N. Radar School, Brigantine, New Jersey, I'm sure he'd get it," the OD said.

"Thank you."

"Not at all." He paused, seemingly debating his next words. "Are you sure I can't help?" His voice rose hopefully.

"No, I'm afraid not. Thank you, sir." She saluted smartly, and then turned, walking rapidly. She felt his eyes on her, and when she stepped over a girder and her skirt was caught by the wind, lifting at the back of her legs, she almost ran headlong away from the ship.

She did not turn, but she knew the OD was smiling.

* * *

There is something completely desolate and forsaken about a seashore resort in winter, Masters thought. He looked out over the water as the PT boat sped for Brigantine Island. Beyond the waves rushing white and green against the sides of the boat, he could see the lobster joint that crouched alongside the boat landing. Far down the stretch of tan beach, the Steel Pier jutted out into the water, a huge structure that insinuated its presence on the seascape.

He lighted a cigarette and watched the coxswain at the wheel of the boat. He handles the boat well, Masters thought. And this was a damned fine jamming run. The boys are learning. If the boys back at the hotel did as well with the junk we threw them, we're going to be all right. He puffed on the cigarette complacently and turned his eyes to the heavy gray clouds piling up on the horizon. Rain will be just dandy, he thought. Rain'll ground the B-26, and that'll shoot our night air exercise all to hell.

He flipped the cigarette over the side when the boat nudged the island's dock. He counted heads as his radarmen leaped ashore, and then he returned the ensign's salute and gave him permission to shove off. He watched while the crew of the boat, led by the young ensign CO, edged the boat away from the dock, and then swung it around in a wide, foaming arc out onto the water. He began walking back to the hotel with his men then.

The airmail special-delivery letter was waiting in his room.

He threw his cap onto his bunk and shrugged out of his coat, and then he picked up the letter. It was postmarked late Saturday, in Norfolk, Virginia, and this was Monday. The name J.R. Dvorak was in the left-hand corner, and for a moment the initials threw him. When he realized it was from Jean, he ripped open the flap rapidly, unfolded the letter, and sat on the edge of his bunk to read it.

She had a neat hand, he noticed. He put the letter in his lap, lighted a cigarette, and then leaned back against the pillow, picking up the letter again.

Dear Chuck:

I'd have written sooner, but I wasn't sure in my own mind exactly what I was going to do until just a little while ago. I'm sure now, and I want you to know about it because I'm still not certain about how all this will turn out.

I think I've found the man who murdered Claire Cole and Schaefer. I think, too, that he killed a pharmacist's mate named Greg Barter, here at the hospital.

I know this will shock you, and I do wish you were here, Chuck, because I feel so desperately alone, and I'm not even sure I'm proceeding the right way. But I have to find out if he is the right man, and there's only one way of doing that.

He came into the hospital with catarrhal fever, or at least that's what they diagnosed. He was placed on my ward, and I treated him just as I would any other patient, until just recently. He became very friendly, and he is really a charming sort of persistent person, Chuck, and I can see how he'd be able to sway a woman. He swayed *me*, at any rate, and I hope you know I was waiting for you to write or call me, but when you didn't I just didn't know what to do and he seemed like a very nice person, so I hope you understand. I went out with him last night, Chuck. He told me that he'd dated another nurse, and I remembered then that he was one of the men you suspected.

He wouldn't tell me who she was, Chuck, and I didn't want to press him, because if he is the man, then I'm a little afraid of him. He asked me to go with him to Wilmington, which is where Claire went, you know, and he called me this morning, and I told him yes, I'd go.

I don't know if I'm doing the right thing or not, Chuck, but it seemed to me I could find out if I were alone with him again, and it seemed to me that a murderer should be revealed, shouldn't he? Chuck dearest, shouldn't I take the chance if it means exposing him?

Well, we're leaving Norfolk Monday morning at 8:15, and we'll be in Wilmington at 3:42 in the afternoon. I don't know where he's taking me, and I don't know what I'll do when I find out whether or not he's the killer, but even if I can't get anything out of him, maybe I can find out where he took Claire in Wilmington, and even that is a start. I think this is the right way, but I wanted you to know about it just in case anything should go wrong.

His name, Chuck, as you probably know by now . . .

15

MASTERS READ THE NAME RAPIDLY, AND THEN CRUSHED
the letter in his fist. Of course. Jesus Christ, of course. It
had to be. It couldn't be otherwise; not now, it couldn't.
He got to his feet quickly.

What was today? Sunday? No, no, it was Monday already! Then . . . oh, Jesus, they were already on the train
to Wilmington! Could he get to them? Could, hell! He *had*
to!

He left his room and rang for the elevator in the hallway.
When the car came, he got in quickly, taking it up to the
Commanding Officer's floor. He walked rapidly into the
office, gave the yeoman there his name, and asked to see
the CO immediately on an urgent matter. He looked at his
watch and then paced the floor anxiously while he waited.
The time was 1036.

At 1041, he was ushered into Lieutenant Commander
Whitley's office. The CO rose, extended his hand, and
shook Master's hand warmly.

"Sit down," he said, "sit down. Been keeping you
hopping this past week, haven't we?"

"Yes, sir," Masters said. "Sir, I'd like permission to
go ashore immediately on a matter of extreme impor-
tance."

Whitley cocked his head and stared at Masters. "Important, huh?" he asked.

"Yes, sir. Extremely so."

"And you have to go into Atlantic City, eh? Well, I
can't see any reason why—"

"Not Atlantic City, sir. Wilmington. Delaware."

"Wilmington?" Whitley was already shaking his head.

"Sir, I have to—"

"I can't grant that permission, Masters. You should know that."

"Why not, sir? This is—"

"I can grant you liberty, sure. But Wilmington! Masters, you're under orders from the captain of your ship. Those orders sent you to Brigantine. I can't countermand those orders."

"But, sir—"

"If it's that important, get a wire off to your skipper. If he replies with permission, you can take off at once, of course."

"Thank you, sir." Masters rose and started for the door. He turned abruptly, remembering Whitley. "I'm sorry, sir. I—"

"Go right ahead, Masters. Good luck."

He sent the wire from the pay telephone on the main floor, and then he began waiting for the reply. The answer came at 1251. He tore open the envelope frantically.

CAPTAIN GLENBURNE AND EXECUTIVE OFFICER ASHORE ON LEAVE. AS SENIOR OFFICER ABOARD CANNOT COUNTERMAND ORDERS OF COMMANDING OFFICER IN HIS ABSENCE. SORRY CHUCK. YOU'LL HAVE TO SWEAT IT OUT.
ARTHUR L. CARLUCCI
LT., USN

He cursed Carlucci and then he cursed the Navy, and then he cursed Whitley for not being decent enough to grant him a sort of extended liberty without running into any "countermanding" red tape. And after he had cursed out everyone he could think of, he went up to his room and packed a bag, and then he began looking for Ensign Andrew Brague, the new meathead communications man they'd given him.

When he found him, he said, "I'm shoving off, Brague. You're in command."

"Sir?"

"I'm going to Wilmington. I'm jumping ship, goddamnit. Keep it under your lid until I'm off the island. Then you can scream all you want to."

"But . . . but, sir . . ."

"So long, chum."

It was 1320 before he got to the station. He asked at the information booth for the next train to Wilmington, and they told him it would leave at 1355, making a stop in North Philly at 1440, and leaving there at 1454 to arrive at Wilmington at 1532.

Fifteen-thirty-two! Ten minutes earlier than the train Jean would be on. He could be waiting for them at the station in Wilmington when they arrived. He thanked his guardian angel, bought a ticket, and then looked for a pay phone. It had suddenly occurred to him that perhaps Jean had changed her mind at the last moment, in which case he'd want to get another wire off to Carlucci, asking him to restrict his man to the ship. He haggled with the operator until he made it clear he wanted the nurses' quarters on the base, and then was told he'd have to wait until they had a free line. He asked the operator to ring him back, and then he sat in the booth and watched the black hands of the clock on the wall march steadily toward traintime. At 1321 the phone rang, and he hastily snatched the receiver from its hook.

"Hello," he shouted.

"I can make your call now, sir."

"Well, Jesus, make it!"

He heard some interoperator gobbledygook, and then the honeyed Southern tones of the Norfolk operator came onto the line. His operator gave her the number, and there was a series of clicks on the line, and then the steady on-and-off hum that told him the line was busy. He nearly rammed his fist against the wall of the booth, and then the operator said, "I'm sorry, sir, the line is busy."

"This is an emergency, operator. Can't you cut in?"

"I'm sorry, sir. If you'll wait, I'll ring you back."

He looked at the clock on the wall. "Operator, I'm getting aboard a train in . . . eleven minutes. Make it fast, will you?"

"I'll do my best, sir."

He hung up and waited, and he heard the train pull into the station, saw the passengers in the waiting room straggle out to meet it. At 1330 the phone rang again, and he grabbed the receiver eagerly.

"Yes?"

"I have your call now, sir."

"Thank you."

"Hello?"

"Hello, Jean?"

"I beg your pardon."

He realized he hadn't made a person-to-person call, and he rapidly said, "Get me Jean Dvorak on the double, miss. This is an emergency."

"Yes, sir," the voice on the other end said, recognizing authority.

He waited for three minutes, and at 1333 she came on the line again.

"Sir?"

"Yes?"

"I'm sorry, sir, but Miss Dvorak is not aboard, sir."

"When did she leave?"

"Early this morning, sir."

Outside, on the track, he heard the conductor yell, "Board! *Board!*"

"Thanks," he said, and then he hung up rapidly, ran out of the booth, and hopped onto the train just as it started rolling out of the station.

The train pulled into North Philly at 1440, as scheduled. It was supposed to leave again at 1454, after a five-minute wait in the station. It did not leave until 1520, twenty-six minutes behind schedule. When Masters arrived in Wilmington, at 1600 that afternoon, the train from Norfolk had already arrived and left again.

Masters searched the station for Jean frantically. At 1605 he resigned himself to the fact that she was somewhere in Wilmington with a murderer as her escort.

Where? He wondered.

And then he began looking.

They sat on opposite sides of the small table. The table had been set up by a bellboy who assumed the couple in 201 were honeymooners. The waiter who brought the two steak dinners and the bottle of champagne had assumed the same thing. He had served them with polite aloofness, having learned long ago that honeymooners did not relish conversation or any other kind of intrusion. He had left them quietly and unobtrusively, closing the door gently behind them.

The two plates rested on the small table now. Jean's steak was hardly touched. His steak had been devoured in apparent good appetite, and his crossed fork and steak knife rested on his bone-cluttered platter now.

"Drink your champagne," he said.

She reached for her glass, her hand trembling. She put the rim to her lips and took a tiny sip.

"More," he said. "Champagne is good for you."

"I don't want to get dizzy."

"I get dizzy just looking at you," he said. He paused. "Why don't you take off your jacket?"

"It's . . . it's a little chilly in here."

"I'll keep you warm," he said, smiling. "Go ahead, take it off."

She unbuttoned her jacket, conscious of the thrust of her breasts, and his eyes coveting them.

"That's a pretty blouse," he said.

"Thank you."

"Are you nervous?"

"Y . . . yes."

"Don't be. We didn't have any trouble registering, did we?"

"No. How did you know about this place?"

"The David Blake? I just knew it, that's all."

"Did you bring that . . . that other nurse here?"

"What other nurse?" he asked, smiling. "I don't know what you're talking about."

"You said you'd dated another nurse."

"Oh, her."

"Did you bring her here?"

He shoved back his chair and walked around the table, standing behind her chair, putting his hands on her shoulders. "What do you care about any other nurse for?" he asked softly.

"I . . ." She tilted her head coyly, trying to smile, the smile giving the lie to the hammering fear within her. "I guess I'm just jealous."

"Well, it certainly wouldn't make you happier to know I brought anyone else here, would it?"

"Yes, I think it would."

"Why?"

"I don't know. I guess I want reassurance. I'm still afraid someone will . . . will catch us."

"Don't worry about that," he said. He bent down and kissed the side of her neck, and she shivered involuntarily. His hands were still tight on her shoulders. "Come on," he said. "Finish your drink."

She lifted the glass again, not drinking. *"Did* you bring her here?" she insisted.

"Yes. If it'll make you feel more secure, yes I did."

"And . . . and no one found out?"

"Not a soul."

"Was she from the hospital at Norfolk? The other nurse, I mean?"

"You talk too much, Jean," he said, and he pulled her out of the chair, his arms encircling her, his mouth reaching for hers.

He was unfamiliar with Wilmington, and so he didn't know where to go, didn't know where they could have gone. And, not knowing where to go, where to look, Masters felt a futile sense of desperation. Time was a trap, and he was enmeshed in the whirling, grinding gears. Time tried to crush him, and there was nothing he could do against time, nothing he could do against the steadily advancing hands and the knowledge that she was alone with *him* somewhere. The clock on the station wall grinned at him with evil intent, and then the smaller replica on his wrist when he left the depot, the steady tick-tick, the hands biting into the face of the watch, ripping off minutes, steadily advancing, and he didn't know where to go.

You walk toward the center of town, he thought.

You have to evolve some sort of plan, he figured. You have to plan or you get crushed in the wheels of time. But what's my plan? How do I stop a murderer when I don't even know where he is? Where, *where?* A big hotel, a small hotel? A rooming house? A motel on the outskirts of town? A friend's apartment somewhere in town? Where? Oh, for Christ's sake, where?

He stopped a passerby, and he asked about hotels and rooming houses and motels, and he came up with a mental list, and then he kept walking toward the center of town thinking, I'll take them as I come to them. I can't bother with any special kind of order now. Time is my trap, but time can be my ally if I work this right. I'll walk and I'll stop at each one I pass on any street. And then I'll take the next street, and the next, and maybe, maybe . . .

He quickened his pace and ducked his head against the wind.

Jean stood in the circle of his arms and turned her head, avoiding his lips. "No," she said. "Couldn't we . . . couldn't we talk a little first?"

"Well, honey, we haven't got all day, you know. We've got to get a train at—"

"I know, but talk to me. Please."

"Sure," he said, sighing. "What do we talk about?"

"Your . . . your other nurse."

"Oh, Jesus!"

"Was she from Norfolk?"

"Yes, she was from Norfolk," he said wearily.

"Did I know her?"

"Aw, come on, Jean," he pleaded, "what's the sense in this?" He took her hand and pulled her to a chair with him. He sat abruptly, yanking her onto his lap. He tilted her back then, and his mouth clamped down onto hers, his lips moving savagely. She tried to pull away from him, but his grip was strong, and she could barely move in the tightness of his embrace. There was real fear inside her now, a pounding, staccato fear that drummed in her blood. She shouldn't have come here. No, she knew that now. This was senseless, this was idiotic. He could . . . he could . . .

His hand dropped to the top button of her blouse, and suddenly dropped again, and again, and she looked down to see that the three top buttons were unbuttoned. She could see the dark valley between her breasts, and his hand moving swiftly on the blouse, button after button.

"No!" she said sharply, and he glanced up quickly, surprised. "I . . . Let me do it myself," she added hastily.

He smiled and released her. "All right," he said.

She got off his lap and walked across the room, the table with the empty plates and glasses, the soiled forks and steak knives between them.

How many buttons are there on this blouse? she wondered. How long will it take me? Oh, God, what do I do next?

"A blonde," Masters said. "A pretty blonde. With a man."

The man with the eyeshade studied him curiously.

"Can you hear me?" Masters asked, his voice rising.

"I c'n hear yuh, awright," the man with the eyeshade said.

"Well, did they register?"

"Um," the man said.

"They did?" Masters asked eagerly.

"No, didn't say that, young feller. Just trying to think."

"Did they? For Christ's sake, did they?"

The man with the eyeshade blew his nose. He folded the handkerchief carefully, put it into his back pocket, and then cleared his throat. "Nope," he said. "Don't believe so. You lookin' for a room, I think I might be able to—"

Masters turned from the desk and walked through the small lobby and then down the steps onto the sidewalk. The elm in front of the small establishment cast a long shadow on to the pavement, and he glanced unconsciously toward the sun, saw it poised close to the horizon.

Darkness soon, he thought. Night.

He glanced in both directions.

Where now? Which next?

At the end of the street, he saw a small swinging sign with the legend "Rooms for Rent."

He began walking rapidly, his shadow darting before him, his strides devouring the long stretches of concrete.

How many has it been now? That woman with the wart, and then the starched clerk with the carnation, and the old man who was reading the newspaper and who wouldn't talk business until we went inside to the desk, and the pretty brunette in black (a recent widow?), and now this one with the eyeshade and the green shadow over his face. How many have there been, and how many more do I hit before I find them?

Give me radar now, give me a radar set that can tear down these goddamn walls and see what he's doing to her, and where!

"Rooms for Rent," the sign read. Masters climbed the steps rapidly.

Her fingers trembled on the buttons of her blouse. He watched her from across the room. "Did I know this nurse?" she asked again.

"You're beautiful, Jean," he whispered.

She finished unbuttoning the blouse, and it hung open

over the protective nylon of her slip. She felt absolutely naked, his eyes hot upon her.

"Why don't you take it off?" he suggested.

She hesitated, and he made a slight movement, as if he would rise from the chair to help her. She slipped out of the blouse then, folded it neatly, stalling, and then draped it over the back of a chair.

"Did . . . did I know her?" she asked again. Answer me, she pleaded silently. Please, please answer me!

"The skirt," he said gently. "Shall I help you?"

"No! No, it's all right." The skirt. One button, and a short zipper. Only a button and a zipper. Oh, my God.

Her hand moved to the button, and she felt it come undone, and then the zipper slid down, almost of its own volition, and the skirt slithered past her thighs like a live thing. She felt the static electricity as the wool caught at the nylon of her slip, and then the skirt was mounded at her ankles, and she stepped out of it quickly as he came out of the chair.

She stood in her slip and watched him advance, aware of the floor lamp in the corner, knowing the lamp was throwing harsh light through the sheer nylon, knowing she might just as well be stark naked, seeing the emotion flooding up into his eyes. She backed away a pace, involuntarily, and then, as if she could think of no other protection from his gaze and his advance, she shouted, *"Did I know the other nurse?"*

The table was between them now, and he stopped on the other side of it and stared at her curiously, and all the fear crawled up into her throat until she thought she would be sick.

"What do you mean by that?" he asked.

"The other nurse. I wanted to know—"

"You said 'did'! What did you mean by that? Why 'did'? Why past tense?"

Her hand went to her throat. "I—I didn't mean anything. I just thought—"

"Why didn't you say, '*Do* I know the other nurse?' Answer me, Jean! Goddamnit, answer me!"

She could not speak. He was crouched over the table now, his palms flat, the forks and the steak knives alongside his hands. His eyes were narrow now, and all desire seemed to have fled them.

"Answer me!"

"I . . . I . . ."

"Who sent you to spy on me?" he shouted. "Masters?"

"No! Chuck doesn't—"

"*Chuck,* is it? *Chuck?*" His eyes were wild now. He knew he was in danger, and she could feel the knowledge triggering inside his head, ricocheting off the walls of his skull. He was like an animal now, trapped, and his eyes raked her body angrily, lashing at her.

"What do you know about Claire Cole?" he snapped.

"Nothing."

"What'd she tell you?"

"Nothing, I swear. We were roommates, but she never—"

"Roommates!" He hurled the word across the room, and then his hands moved on the table and one of them closed around the gleaming, razor-sharp steak knife.

The street lights were coming on when Masters entered the lobby of the David Blake. He walked directly to the desk, annoyed when he saw no clerk in attendance. He rapped on the bell, and a small man in a dark-brown suit emerged from the shadows, a smile magically appearing on his face.

"Yes, sir," he said, "may I help you?"

"I'm looking for a girl," Masters said. "She may have—"

The clerk's face clouded. He cocked his head to one side and said, "I'm sorry, Lieutenant, but this isn't that kind of hotel."

Masters slammed his fist onto the desk. "Don't be a

fool!'' he shouted. "She may have registered here, with a man. She's a blonde, very pretty, registered sometime this afternoon."

"Her name, sir?" the clerk asked, flustered.

"They probably used phony names. Did a blonde register with anyone this afternoon? Any time after about four o'clock?"

"Well, we get a lot of guests, sir," the clerk said, plainly miffed. "It would be almost impossible to distinguish one from—"

"A blonde!" Masters shouted. "Look, you idiot, I've been looking all over town, and you're just about the last goddamn stop, and this girl is in danger!"

"We had several blondes this afternoon, sir," the clerk said, a little frightened by the gleam in Masters' eyes.

"With men?"

"One with a man, sir."

"Where?"

"A honeymoon couple, sir."

"*Where*, goddamnit!"

"Surely, sir, you don't want us to disturb a honeymoon couple."

Masters reached across the desk. "What room? Take me up there, or I'll—"

The clerk's eyes popped wide, and his mouth worked fitfully. He reached for the passkey behind him and said, "Y-y-y-yes, sir. This way, sir."

He picked up the knife in a lithe, smooth motion, his hand surrounding the handle intimately.

"Did she tell you about us?"

"No!" Jean said, backing away now, moving across the room in her slip. He followed her relentlessly, his fingers tight around the handle of the knife, and knife deadly cold and poised in his fist.

"Was this Masters' idea? Did he put you onto this? Are you trying to find out if I killed her or not?"

"You . . ." She swallowed and then gulped for air.

"You did kill her, didn't you? You killed her . . . and the others."

He took a fast step toward her, seizing her wrist and swinging her back across the room, onto the bed. Her slip pulled back over her thighs, and he advanced on her with the knife, and then he stopped and looked down at the taut, ribbed tops of her stockings, and his eyes grew reflectively canny, and his mouth quirked into a strange smile.

"Yes," he said softly. "I killed her."

He kept staring at her legs, as if remembering something, remembering it vividly.

"I shouldn't have killed her," he whispered. "All that woman lying on the deck, worthless, dead." His mouth was twitching now, twitching wildly. "It'll be different with you, you bitch! No regrets this time. No eating my heart out afterward! You're going to die, but this time the memory's going to be fresh. This time—"

"No," she screamed. "Please!"

He reached out suddenly, his free hand grasping the front of her slip, yanking her off the bed. She came toward him, her back arching, and then the nylon gave with a rasping screech, and she fell back onto the bed, released, the slip torn to her waist.

Slowly he advanced, wetting his lips, the knife poised and ready.

He must have heard the door, the frantic knocking, and then the harsh splintering sound as the wood ripped free from the lock. But he did not whirl until Masters' voice shouted from the doorway, "Hold it, Jones!"

He whirled and then stepped off on his right foot in one smooth motion, sprinting for the door, the knife high over his head.

"You bastard!" he screamed at Masters, and then the knife came down in a winking arc, and Masters felt fear crackle into his skull. He backed away and stepped to the side, and the blade glittered past his cheek, and then he threw his fist at Jones. He caught the radarman in the stomach, and Jones doubled over, straightening up again when Masters' fist caught him under the jaw. The knife clattered to the floor, and Jones scrabbled for it wildly. Masters took a quick lunge forward, stepping on Jones's hand. The radarman let out a sharp cry, pulling his hand back. Masters kicked the knife into a corner of the room, and then stood over Jones, his fists doubled.

"Get up!" Masters said.

"You got nothing on me!" Jones screamed, crouched near the floor. "You got nothing on me, you bastard!"

"He killed her, Chuck! He admitted it," Jean said from the bed. She seemed suddenly to remember her torn slip. She rose quietly and began putting on her jacket.

"Shut up, you bitch!" Jones snarled, turning toward her. "You ain't going to railroad me. I ain't just come into the Navy yesterday. I know my rights."

"You know it's all over, Jones, don't you?" Masters said quietly. "You know you haven't got a chance in hell."

Jones was silent for a long time. Then he said, "Yeah," and he paused and said, "Yeah," again, and then he shook his head and sat down on the floor abruptly, all fight suddenly drained from him, his head bent, his shoulders slumped.

The clerk peeked timidly around the doorjamb.

"Are . . . are these the people you were looking for?" he asked.

"Yes," Masters said, smiling. "These are the people. You'd better call the police."

The clerk nodded, looking at Jones on the floor, and then at the sheer slip showing below Jean's jacket.

He turned to go, and then he turned back and suddenly said, "You didn't have to break the door, you know!"

16

THEY SAT SIDE BY SIDE AS THE TRAIN SPED FOR ATLANTIC City. He held her hand tightly, as if he never wanted to let it go.

"You should be going in the opposite direction," he said.

"I want to be with you," she answered. "I don't have to be back in Norfolk until tomorrow morning."

"How do you feel?" Masters asked.

"All right. Now." She smiled weakly.

"Were you frightened?"

"Oh, God, yes."

"You're a silly little girl. You should never have gone there alone with him."

"Chuck, it worked out all right, though, didn't it? I mean, we did get him, and that's what counts, isn't it?"

"Not if he'd harmed you. If he'd harmed you—"

She squeezed his hand. "But he didn't."

"No, he didn't. But he could have."

"Yes, but he didn't. I mean . . ." She turned her face toward his and raised her eyes. "You know that, don't you? I mean . . . that he didn't."

"Yes."

She turned her head away from him. "I . . . I thought I liked him, Chuck. In the beginning. Before I suspected."

"All right," he said.

"Are you angry?"

"No."

"You are, I can see that. You have a right to be, you

know. Keeping me waiting like that, not calling, not writing, not anything. You're lucky I didn't marry him or something.''

He smiled. ''I know I am.''

''He was very nice,'' she said petulantly. ''He said very nice things to me.''

''Did he now?''

''Yes, he did. He's a murderer, but I didn't know that.''

''I didn't know, either,'' Masters said. ''Christ, what a fool I was! I had every damn radarman from the *Sykes* with me in Atlantic City. I knew that Jones had gone to the hospital sick before we left, and I never made the connection. I kept thinking it was Daniels, but even that ties in now. He was a married man, and he was playing around, and all his lying was just to cover that up. When I got your letter . . . well, sure, then it all added up. God, was I an idiot!''

''Yes,'' Jean agreed. ''You should have called me.''

''I didn't mean . . .'' He paused and then lifted her chin with his fingers. ''Say, what's the matter with you?''

''Nothing.''

''Did I do anything wrong?''

''No.''

''Well, what—''

''You haven't even said . . . you haven't . . . Can't you see I love you?''

''Why, sure I can,'' he said, surprised.

''Then . . . then . . . why haven't you even . . . even . . .'' She seemed ready to cry. She shook her head, freeing her chin from his fingers.''

''I haven't even *what?*'' he asked.

''Said you love me or . . .''

''I love you,'' he said. ''I love you, Jean.''

''. . . or kissed me, or held me, or . . .''

His arms were suddenly around her. He pulled her to him and lifted her chin, and she saw his mouth coming closer to hers and she said, ''Chuck! The conductor! The passeng—''

"The hell with them," he answered, and he kissed her gently and then put his cheek against hers, and he could feel the smile on her mouth when her cheek moved upward against his.

"You looked mighty pretty in your slip," he whispered.

"I know," she answered, and he pulled his face back from hers, surprised. The small smile was still on her mouth, and her happiness glistened in her eyes.

"I meant . . . in the hotel, when your slip—" he started awkwardly.

"I know," she said again, and this time he was really surprised, because there was no blush on her face at all, only a womanly contentment and peace. He kissed her again, just for the hell of it, and he wondered if Commander Glenburne would perform a wedding ceremony aboard the *Sykes,* and then he wondered if he'd need the Navy's official permission to take a wife, and how many forms would have to be filled out, and whether or not . . .

And then he simply concentrated on kissing her.